BROUGHT TO ACCOUNT

When Lauren Chapman is 'let go' from her job at a greengrocer's, her boss encourages her to take a position with a local accountancy firm, Northcott and Company. She does so reluctantly — but when the owner of the company is attacked and left for dead in his office, Lauren is the first person to find him. How is her late mother involved in the mystery? And will a budding romance blossom between her and handsome co-worker Conor Maguire — or is he trying to hide his part in the crime?

Books by Paula Williams
in the Linford Romance Library:

PLACE OF HEALING
FINDING ANNABEL
MOUNTAIN SHADOWS
STORM CHASER
MOUNTAIN ROMANCE

PAULA WILLIAMS

BROUGHT
TO ACCOUNT

Complete and Unabridged

LINFORD
Leicester

First published in Great Britain in 2017

First Linford Edition
published 2018

A catalogue record for this book is available
from the British Library.

ISBN 978–1–4448–3815–2

Published by
F. A. Thorpe (Publishing)
Anstey, Leicestershire

Set by Words & Graphics Ltd.
Anstey, Leicestershire
Printed and bound in Great Britain by
T. J. International Ltd., Padstow, Cornwall

This book is printed on acid-free paper

1

'I'm warning you, Bradley. I'm going to the press. Or maybe even the police. You're not getting away with this. I — '

'Are you threatening me?' Bradley Northcott's cold voice was a stark contrast to the angry one he cut across. 'Because I don't care to be threatened. I've said what I have to say. Now get out — and close the door on your way.'

But although Bradley was outwardly calm, inside he was seething. *Some people,* he thought. *You try to help them, and what happens? At the first sign of trouble, they start bleating they want out.* It wasn't meant to be like this.

But this was exactly how it was meant to be. It was what he'd worked for, planned for, waited for ever since the beginning. It was that close now, he could almost smell it. See the noughts in his carefully hidden bank account. Hear the sounds of the waves lapping against the luxury yacht waiting for him in the Bahamas. Far away from this dreary little town in this dreary little country. And, more to the point, far, far away from the grasping hands of Isobel, his greedy, never satisfied, soon-to-be ex-wife.

And they thought they were going to bring all that crashing down? Over his dead body.

He gave a small exclamation of annoyance as he realised the papers on his desk had become fractionally disarranged. He hated disorder of any kind, but especially here in his work environment. He straightened the papers after first making sure they were still in their original order and moved his gold-nibbed ultra-expensive fountain pen one centimeter to the right. Brushed an imaginary speck of dust from the highly polished surface of his antique mahogany desk.

'Are you still there?' he said without turning round. 'Because I've said my last word on the subject.'

It was indeed his last word.

He didn't hear it coming, and only briefly felt the crushing blow to the back of his head, which propelled him forward.

Had he had time for one last conscious thought, it would have been one of annoyance that his carefully arranged papers had once again become disarranged. And the blood that was pouring from his gaping head wound would ruin the gold-tooled leather top of his desk.

But for Bradley Northcott, there was no more time.

★ ★ ★

Nine days earlier
'Lauren. In my office now, please,' Councillor Dennis Uppington, known to most residents of the small Somerset market town of Stoneford as Dodgy Den, barked as he stormed through the shop, scattering a display of artfully arranged rhubarb as he did so.

He was heading for the cleaning cupboard. It used to be his bolt hole, a place to which he'd escape when he wanted to listen to *Test Match Special* in peace. But since his elevation to town councillor the previous year, he'd become image-conscious and had started referring to the room as his 'office'. It was about the same time he stopped wearing the hand-knitted cricket sweaters his mother made for him — Den was a lifelong cricket fan — and began sporting a mustard-yellow waistcoat in the mistaken belief that it made him look like a country gentleman.

The truth was, given Den's unfortunate taste for tight trousers and his football-shaped paunch that hung over them, he looked more like Toad of Toad Hall. But nobody, least of all Lauren, was going to tell him that. And she certainly wasn't going to do it in the mood he was in that day.

'Den, there's something I need — ' she began, but stopped mid-sentence at the sound of his howl of outrage. Too late now to say that there was something she needed to tell him. He'd already found it.

'What is that — that animal doing in here?' he bellowed. 'This is a green-grocer's shop, in case you hadn't noticed. Not a home for waifs and strays.'

'Dooley's not a waif and stray,' Lauren said. 'And please don't shout because he's — '

But it was obviously her day for not finishing her sentences. This time, it was Dooley who interrupted her as he began barking at Den and advancing on him, hackles raised, his small razor-sharp teeth bared. Nobody had thought to tell Dooley he was a small dog, scarcely larger than a rabbit. In his mind, he was the size and temperament of a Rottweiler with attitude.

Den jumped back, slammed the door of his 'office' shut, and rounded on Lauren. 'You and I need to have a talk,' he said, forced to raise his voice above the sound of Dooley hurling himself at the door. 'Can't you shut him up? He's going to knock the door down in a minute.'

'It's because he can hear us,' Lauren said in a low voice, in the vain hope that it would encourage Den to do the same. 'And you've been shouting. Dooley's very sensitive to people shouting. It makes him feel threatened.'

'*He* feels threatened? I'm the one who's being threatened here. And in my own office, too. It's beyond outrageous,' Den roared. He then made a huge effort and dropped his voice to a hoarse whisper. 'Come into the shop,' he hissed. 'That's probably the one place we won't be interrupted. Least of all by any customers. Goodness knows the place is like a ghost town this morning.'

'Look, I'm sorry about the dog,' Lauren said as she followed him along the narrow corridor and back into the shop. 'He belongs to Elsie Thornton. Well, not really. He doesn't actually belong to anyone since poor old Peggy, that's his owner, died, but — '

'I don't need the dog's biography,' Den muttered.

'Elsie was desperate,' Lauren went

6

on. 'She's only popped into the bank, but they refused to let Dooley in after the last incident. I mean, you wouldn't be very happy if someone stood on your paw, would you? And the guy was making an awful fuss about a pair of jeans that were pretty scruffy to start with. Ripped jeans are quite a fashion statement now. And there was no need to ban Dooley from the premises. Talk about the caring bank. No wonder there's a banking crisis. If they — '

'You're fired,' Den cut in, his face as pink as the rhubarb that was still scattered across the floor.

Lauren started to laugh as she bent down to pick up the rhubarb. 'You've got it wrong, Den. If you're trying to do an impression of Alan Sugar, you should at least get the body language right. You're supposed to point your finger and — '

'This is no joke, Lauren. I mean it. I'm letting you go.'

Lauren stared at him. There was something about the set of his mouth, the way his eyes wouldn't meet hers. Suddenly she didn't feel like laughing anymore. In the six years she'd been working for Den, he'd threatened her with the sack many times, but never really meant it. This was just another of those times — wasn't it?

'How do you mean, letting me go?' she asked. 'As in sacked? I don't understand — '

'I'm not exactly sacking you,' he mumbled. 'Well, yes, I suppose I am in a way.'

'In what way, exactly?'

'No, I'm not sacking you. Not really. But yes, I am letting you go.'

'Letting me go? But that's just another way of saying I'm fired.' Lauren's heart was pounding as with exaggerated care she placed the rhubarb back on the display while she forced herself to stay calm and think. 'Look, Den, I'm sorry about Dooley. I honestly didn't think you'd mind. It was only for a couple of minutes. And listen, he's calmed down now we've moved away from the door and you've stopped shouting. And if it's about those soggy tomatoes, I couldn't let Elsie buy them, not with this morning's delivery still in the stock room, could I? The poor old soul.'

But even as she spoke, Lauren could see it wasn't about soggy tomatoes. And if Elsie Thornton heard her referring to her as a poor old soul, she'd probably handbag her. Elsie was small and prickly with hair like a washed-out Brillo pad; and if gossip ever became an Olympic sport, she'd be a dead cert for a gold medal.

'Elsie was very good to me and Dad after Mum died,' Lauren said with a horrible sinking feel that whatever she said was not going to make a scrap of difference. But she said it anyway. 'I couldn't pass off yesterday's soggy tomatoes on her, could I, now?'

'Why don't you simply give the stuff away?' Den growled. 'That way I'll go broke sooner, and the poor old soul as you call her will have to spend her widow's mite on a taxi to the supermarket, where she'll be getting last month's tomatoes that were grown in the Gobi desert.'

'I don't think they grow tomatoes in the Gobi desert,' Lauren tried to point out but Den wasn't to be distracted.

'Wherever. It's bad enough the supermarkets squeezing me to death without my staff doing it as well.'

'I'm sorry.' Lauren gave him her best, most conciliatory smile. 'Look, would you like me to do your VAT return for you to make up for it? It's due next week. I'll take it home with me and do it over the weekend and won't even claim the overtime for doing it.'

'I can manage, thank you,' he said stiffly.

That was when Lauren finally realised Den was really, really serious. An offer to do the VAT had got her out of trouble on more than one occasion, but it wasn't working that day. As for her offer to work for nothing . . .

'Then if it's not Dooley or the soggy

tomatoes, at least tell me why,' she said. 'I don't understand.'

Since he'd got co-opted onto Stanford Town Council last year, Den had been planning what he was going to do when it was his 'turn' to be mayor. In preparation for his mayoral stint, he'd taken to addressing everyone like he was doing a party political broadcast. He cleared his throat and puffed out his chest.

'The economic downturn is having a devastating effect on the retail sector,' he began in his best mayor-in-waiting voice. 'These out-of-town superstores — '

'I've already said I'm sorry about the tomatoes,' she said in a vain attempt to cut things short.

'This isn't about tomatoes.' He pushed his hand through what he still thought was a full head of hair and in doing so dislodged his comb-over that slipped across one eye, making him look like a slightly manic pirate. Lauren looked away quickly, sensing a snort of laughter would be inappropriate. By the time she'd recovered enough to be sure she wouldn't

11

laugh, he'd moved on. But she didn't feel like laughing when it finally dawned on her where his wittering about economic downturns, cost-cutting and falling sales were leading.

'You're serious, aren't you?' She looked at him in stunned disbelief. 'You really are sacking me.'

Den's face went as purple as the stuff he carefully labelled *Mum's Homemade Pickled Cabbage*, which had probably been pickled by someone's mum in a factory in some far-distant country. But not by Den's, who, since her son became a councillor, was in Elsie's words far too 'hooty-tooty' to pickle cabbage.

'Weren't you listening?' Den said. 'That's what I meant when I said I wasn't exactly sacking you but letting you go. I prefer to call it a career advancement. You're a bright woman, Lauren. You could be doing so much better for yourself than weighing out spuds for a few batty old pensioners.'

'Have you been talking to my dad?'

This was beginning to feel horribly like the conversation she had with her father two or three times every week.

'No. But he only wants the best for you, same as me, and obviously feels the same way about your employment prospects as I do. So here's the plan. You know Bradley Northcott, the accountant, don't you?'

Of course she knew him, unfortunately. Since Den had become a councillor, he and Bradley would spend hours holed up in Den's office cooking up one scheme or another. All of them dodgy, no doubt.

Bradley Northcott was a neat, fussy little man with gold-rimmed glasses. He had a loud braying voice and an ego the size of Manchester. He also had a sleazy way of looking at Lauren that made her feel he was peering down her top, even when she was wearing an up-to-the-neck yellow tabard with *Peas and Cues — your friendly local greengrocer* spelt out in luminous orange lettering across her chest.

She pulled her tabard closer to her neck while Den went on about how he'd told Bradley 'what a whizz' she was with figures and how she was the answer to his staffing crisis.

'So you said I could go and work for him? Just like that?' Now that the first shock was over, Lauren could feel a coil of anger snaking around her insides. 'Like, it never occurred to you to ask me how I felt about it?'

'No, no, Lauren. You've got it all wrong. I'm acting in your best interests, just like I've always done. It's the career opportunity of a lifetime,' he said hastily, a nervous smile twitching his lips. 'Your first step on the corporate ladder. Who knows how far you could go? Like I told Bradley, you're a clever woman, with all those exams. And totally wasted here.'

Once again he was beginning to sound like Lauren's dad. He was always fretting about how working in a greengrocer's was a waste of her A-levels. But the truth was, they meant much more to him — and now, it seemed, to Den as well — than they ever had to her. Her mother, Lou, had been diagnosed with cancer three days after Lauren had finished sitting her A-levels, and by the time the exam results came out, the illness had advanced with such cruel swiftness that Lauren didn't even want to open the envelope, least of all celebrate at the sight of those three grade As.

Before her illness, Lou had owned a craft shop next door to Peas and Cues, which was how she'd known Den was looking for Saturday help. Lauren, who was fifteen at the time, applied for the job and got it. She left school soon after Lou died, and that was when Den asked her if she'd like to work for him full-time. And she'd been with him ever since. Since she was fifteen years old, for goodness sake! And now he was 'letting her go'. Just like that. How dare he!

She pulled her tabard off, slammed it down on the counter and, rigid with fury, strode to the shop door. 'I've worked for you for six years,' she said. 'And you pass me on to one of your cronies like an unwanted parcel. Well, you can tell Bradley Northcott that this particular parcel has been lost in the post, and he can look someone else to solve his staffing crisis. Because it won't be me.'

'Now, don't be hasty, Lauren. And, like I said, I didn't exactly sack you. It was more — '

'Well, you might not exactly have sacked me,' she cut in. 'But I quit.'

As exit lines, it would have been a perfect one, if she hadn't stepped on a soggy tomato on her way out, sending a shower of squashed tomato shooting up the leg of her favourite skinny jeans. She wrenched open the shop door and hurried out into the street, still hissing, spitting angry. So angry she almost didn't stop when Den called her back.

'Lauren. Please. Wait.' His voice was shrill with anxiety.

She turned back slowly, determined

to make him grovel.

'Would you please take that hell hound out of my office before he breaks the door down?' he asked plaintively. 'And promise me you'll think about Bradley's offer. Talk it over with your dad. Bradley says for you to call into his office and arrange an interview any time to suit yourself.'

2

Conor Maguire was still bristling with fury as he strode along the high street. He shouldn't have walked out like that. But honestly, if he'd stayed in that office a moment longer, he'd have decked the man, so he would.

He checked his stride to skirt around a couple of pigeons that were half-heartedly pecking around an overflowing litter bin. Even they looked depressed, and who could blame them? The first time he'd come to Stoneford, he'd thought what a rundown place it was, and it hadn't changed in the intervening few years. Not for the better, anyway. Just a few more charity shops and a boarded-up pub with a For Sale sign on it.

He should never have come here, that much was certain. But he was never any good at saying no — not to her, anyway. And someone had to bring Bradley

Northcott down. He owed her that, at least.

At the time, he'd jumped at the chance to get out of London, where everything had gone wrong for him. He hated the commute, the noise, the job — and as for coming home to an empty flat, that was the worst of all. London could be the loneliest place in the world, as he'd discovered once Helen moved out. And even though their relationship had long since run its course and she'd done them both a favour by ending it, he still couldn't get used to the emptiness of the flat without her things cluttering up every available space.

So when this job in Somerset came up, it had seemed the ideal chance for him to make the break and move right away. He needed a change. And this was as big a change as you could get. Stoneford's high street, where the only sign of life apart from the pigeons was a young woman walking a small wiry haired-dog, was as far from London's

19

bustling pavements as you could get.

But in fact the woman wasn't walking. She was stepping it out as if in training for the Olympics, her long blond ponytail swinging like a pendulum as she did so. Wherever she was heading, she was in one hell of a hurry — and, from the scowl on her face, she looked about as angry as he felt.

She stopped almost in front of him and was about to cross the road when a white van appeared from nowhere. The angry blast of his horn ripped into the still of the afternoon and sent the pigeons flapping skyward in alarm.

'Tired of living, love?' the van driver shouted as he roared off.

She stepped back quickly, and in doing so tripped over the dog, whose lead was now tangled around her feet. Then she stumbled and almost fell. Managing to save herself, she dropped her handbag in the process; a misnomer if ever there was one, given that it was the size of a small suitcase. She cursed as its contents spilled across the pavement.

A couple of tomatoes splatted at Conor's feet, just missing his shoes. He picked the least squished one up. 'Yours, I presume?' he asked, holding it by the stalk. 'Although I don't suppose you'll be wanting it now.'

'I certainly do. Thanks.' She took the tomato, then threw it with impressive accuracy at the van, now held up at the traffic lights. It hit the rear doors with a satisfying thud.

Conor's approving 'Shot!' earned him a brief flicker of a smile before she bent down to pick up the rest of her scattered belongings. Her legs, in those tight, skinny jeans, were long, slim and tomato-stained, while her eyes were the colour of the sea and fringed with long sweeping lashes. Thanks to whatever or whoever had made her so angry even before her encounter with White Van Man, they were now the colour of a very stormy sea. But, he mused, they were the kind of eyes a man could lose himself in. Not this man, obviously. He was off women forever. Even though he'd also noticed her long, slender fingers and clocked that they were ringless.

'Can I help you with that?' he asked.

Her 'no thanks' was muffled as she scrabbled around his feet, scooping everything except the other tomatoes back into the bag, while her dog obviously thought it was a new sort of game and yelped with excitement as he did everything he could to get in her way.

Conor's earlier bad mood evaporated as he watched the whole thing with evident enjoyment. She was without doubt the best thing he'd seen since arriving in the town. But there was no room in his life at the moment for complications. And there was something about the set of her chin and the straight way she'd looked at him with those stormy green-grey eyes that warned him this woman could be complicated with a capital C.

'You missed that.' He pointed at a small well-worn hairbrush that had ended up over by the bin. 'Is it yours?'

'No,' she said shortly, then obviously regretted her sharpness, because she suddenly smiled. It was like the sun coming out. 'Sorry. It's not been the best of days,' she went on. 'What I meant to say was no, it's not mine. But thanks for asking. I'll just pop it in the bin. Honestly, the rubbish some people leave around. You wouldn't credit it, would you?'

'Indeed not.' Conor smiled back, gave himself a mental shake and forced himself to walk on. He wasn't here to chat up the locals, however appealing. Or complicated. He was here to do a job, keep himself to himself, and then move on. That was the deal.

* * *

'Going somewhere special, Mrs Northcott?'

Isobel Northcott bit back an exclamation of annoyance. What was it with hairdressers that they felt obliged to chatter on all the time they were working? Why couldn't they just get on with what they were paid to do and leave their clients in peace? Even the dog-eared copies of *Vogue* were more entertaining than listening to Sandra Wilde wittering on about last night's *Eastenders*, or whatever it was she was going on about.

'Not really,' Isobel said as her heart gave a little lift of excitement. It was true she wasn't going anywhere special. But she was certainly hoping to *meet* someone special. In fact, she was sure of it. It was in her diary. Antonio, 10.30 tomorrow morning.

Just thinking about him made her heart race in a way that it hadn't raced for — well, forever, if she was honest. There was no way Bradley had ever made her feel the way she was feeling now, that was for sure. The closest anyone had come would have been when she'd fallen deeply in love with Queen's Brian May when she was twelve. And even that was probably because her mother couldn't stand him. She'd loved Bradley, though, and couldn't hustle Isobel down the aisle quick enough.

'You and Mr Northcott going any-where nice for your holidays?' Sandra went on as she applied hair colour to Isobel's roots. If it hadn't been for Antonio and those grey hairs she'd found this morning, there was no way she'd have booked herself into this awful place. Wilde and Wonderful. What sort of a name was that for a hairdressers, for heaven's sake? Did the locals in this dreary little town have a competition for the corniest shop name? If so, this place would give Peas and Cues, the greengrocer's further down the street, a run for its money.

Needs must, though, she thought with a sigh. Jean-Paul, her regular hairdresser, was on holiday, and she couldn't afford to wait for his return. And what harm could Sandra do? It wasn't like she was letting the woman anywhere near her hair with a pair of scissors. Jean-Paul would have a fit if anyone did that.

'Sorry? I was miles away. What did you say?' Isobel asked when it became obvious that Sandra had asked her something and was waiting for an answer.

'I asked if you and Mr Northcott are going somewhere nice for your holidays this year.'

Isobel smiled. A slow, secret smile that warmed her inside. 'Maybe Portugal.' She spoke softly, talking more to herself than answering Sandra's question. 'Yes, I rather think I fancy Portugal this year. From what I hear, it's a beautiful country.'

'And I'm sure Mr Northcott will find himself the odd golf course or two,' Sandra said with her shrill laugh that set Isobel's teeth on edge. 'Who'd be a golfing widow, eh?'

I would, Isobel thought to herself in a sudden rush of realisation that left her breathless. *In fact, given the choice, I'd be any sort of widow, and the sooner the better.*

26

A widow. How different her life would be if she were. If only it were that easy, like it on TV. You wanted someone eliminated. You made one phone call and that was it. An 'accident' would be arranged.

Bradley would agree to a divorce tomorrow. She knew that only too well. He was no happier with their sham of a marriage than she was. But she knew, as well as she knew her own name, that if they were to divorce, he would leave her penniless.

But if she were a widow ... She closed her eyes and imagined her and Antonio on a wide, sandy Portuguese beach, a light breeze ruffling her hair as they walked along the shoreline. Or maybe wandering hand in hand through the narrow streets of Oporto's Villa Nova, the oldest part of the town with its higgledy-piggledy roofs and walls decorated with colourful ceramic tiles. Then later sitting in the sun, sipping crisp chilled vinho verde and watching the boats make their way up the broad sweep of the river Douro while he told her the history of that fascinating city. She'd looked Oporto up on the internet, and it certainly looked wonderful.

The last time they'd spoken, Antonio had told her about the quinta that his grandparents still farmed way up in the Douro valley.

'It sounds amazing,' she'd said. 'I'd love to see it.'

His dark eyes had softened as he smiled down at her. 'One day, you come visit to Portugal. I show you.'

At his words, spoken in his hesitant, broken English, her heart had leapt like a schoolgirl's encountering her first crush. But that was just what it felt like. Like she was in love for the first time in her life. And maybe she was. Certainly she'd never felt like this about Bradley. Not even when she'd first started working for him as his secretary all those years ago.

And she was beginning to think that maybe, just maybe, Antonio felt the same way about her. Certainly, he always made a point of singling her out, of paying her particular attention. Which was why she didn't want to mess things up; why she wanted to look her very best when she saw him tomorrow — and that didn't include grey hairs. She thought she might wear —

'Well, did you see that? My life, that was a close thing!' Once again, Sandra Wilde's irritating voice broke into her daydreams. 'That woman just stepped out right in front of that van. Oh, for pity's sake, will you look who it is — it's Lauren. That's my son's girlfriend. What on earth was she thinking of, stepping into the road without looking? I'll be having words with her, you see if I don't.'

Isobel bit back the comment that she'd prefer Sandra's attention to be focused one hundred percent on her hair rather than what was going on in the street outside. She didn't want to upset her and end up with badger-stripes in her hair.

She flicked a glance at the young

woman who'd caught Sandra's attention. Quite attractive; or she could be, if she made more of herself and dressed a bit smarter instead of that scruffy way that young women did these days. That was a half-decent pair of jeans she was wearing, for heaven's sake, but totally ruined by an ugly stain all down one leg. Did young people have no self-respect? Fancy walking around like that. And as for the young man who'd stopped to help her gather up her things, now he was an unusual sight in Stoneford. Dressed in a smart suit, collar and tie, he was certainly easy on the eye. Not that he could hold a candle to Antonio, of course.

'Well now, there's a tasty bit of eye candy to brighten up the day,' Sandra said. 'That has to be that young Irishman who's started working for your husband. I heard he was a looker.'

Isobel didn't even know Bradley had taken on anyone new in the office. But then, he never discussed his work with her; and if he did, she wouldn't listen anyway. What was it they said about boring accountants being a cliché? In Bradley's case, it was no cliché, but perfectly true. The man could bore for England.

'Hey, that was a cracking shot!' Sandra exclaimed as the young woman picked up a tomato and threw it at the white van, which was now waiting at the traffic lights. It hit the rear door with a satisfying splat. 'She always did have a good eye, did our Lauren! And a bit of a temper on her, by the look of it. I'd best warn Scott to watch out. Watch his Peas and Cues.' She went on into a cackle of laughter. 'Peas and Cues, get it? That's where she works. She could — '

But Isobel had stopped listening and was already back in her daydream about Antonio with his finely honed body and those beautiful brown eyes, as dark and sexy as molten chocolate.

3

Lauren cursed herself for being so quick to drop her hairbrush in the bin. Manky it might have been, which was why she hadn't wanted to admit to it being hers, but now she was one of the newly unemployed, she didn't really want to fork out for a new one.

On the other hand, she didn't fancy rooting around in the bin to retrieve it either. If she'd known the guy was going to hurry off like that, she'd have hung on to it.

Elsie Thornton had a saying or three for every situation, and one of her favourites was how clean shoes were the sign of a decent man. As Lauren watched him stride off down the high street, neatly avoiding an elderly man on a mobility scooter as he did so, she conceded that for once Elsie could well be right. Lauren had almost fallen at his feet and had come so close to his highly polished shoes she could almost see her face in them. And when she'd looked up at the rest of him, his formal dark suit and white shirt a marked contrast to her own tomato-stained jeans and faded pink T-shirt, the only word that came to mind was 'wow'.

He was more than decent. He was without doubt the hottest-looking guy to appear in Stoneford high street since they took the poster of Benedict Cumberbatch out of the newsagents' window. As for that accent, it was as soft and gentle as Irish rain, and made a polite enquiry about a squished tomato sound like a poem.

She regretted her abrupt refusal of his offer to help. But the truth was, she'd already gathered up her phone, purse and the supersized packet of jelly babies and was too embarrassed to admit the manky hairbrush belonged to her.

She watched him until he turned into a little alleyway that led to a lovely old

Victorian terrace that was now mainly offices. As she watched him stride off, she fantasised about what she'd say if a miracle happened, and he turned back and asked her if she could recommend a decent restaurant in the town and would she have dinner with him later.

But, of course, miracles didn't happen in Stoneford, she thought sadly, otherwise Harvey Nicks would be where the charity shop for homeless hamsters was, and Jamie Oliver would have revamped the chippie into one of his trendy restaurants. And Dodgy Den wouldn't have sacked her and then had the nerve to pretend he was doing her a stonking great favour.

'Come on, Lauren,' had been his parting shot once she'd gone back for Dooley. 'This could be the best thing to happen to you. With your head for figures, surely you fancy a career in accountancy? You'd love it. You know you will.'

It was true that Lauren enjoyed working with numbers. Maths had been one of her favourite subjects at school; and at one time, before her mother's illness, she'd planned to study it at university. Nevertheless, she found it hard to get excited about debits and credits any more than she could about rhubarb and broccoli. As for working for Bradley Northcott, Stoneford's very own Mr Big . . . She shook her head. Absolutely no way.

'Have you been making a nuisance of yourself again, Dooley?'

Lauren looked up and smiled as she saw Elsie coming towards her. Dooley was more interested in hoovering up one of the splatted tomatoes and ignored her. Elsie and Dooley had an odd sort of relationship. He'd belonged to Peggy, Elsie's elderly neighbour who'd had a bad fall a few months earlier. Elsie had taken the dog in while the old lady was in hospital. But sadly, Peggy died, and Elsie was left with Dooley. She was always saying that she and Dooley did not get on and that she was going to take him to the rehoming centre, but she never did. Lauren thought she actually quite enjoyed having a dog who caused chaos wherever he went. Which he did. Getting banned from the bank was only the latest in a long line of places where Dooley was not welcome. And that included the local vet.

'What took you so long in the bank?' Lauren asked. 'You said without Dooley around to savage the customers, you'd be in and out in five minutes. Were you taken hostage or something?'

Elsie laughed. 'They wouldn't dare,' she said. 'I only got stuck behind that new woman who started in the newsagent's last week, didn't I? Someone had obviously been raiding the kids' money boxes, because the week's takings were all in 10p and 20p pieces; and, of course, there was only one counter open, and the woman took forever to count it all out. I told her that people have better things to do than hang around all day in her bank.'

'Well, some of us do,' Lauren said.

'Anyway, thanks for looking after Dooley,' Elsie said, taking the lead from Lauren. 'Next time, though, I'll take him in with me, whatever they say. It'll get the queue moving a bit quicker if he starts yapping.'

'Or you'll end up getting banned as well as him.'

'Hang on a bit.' Elsie peered closely at her. 'What are you doing out here at this time of day? Don't tell me Dooley started playing up. Or did Dodgy Den finally give you time off for good behaviour? That man works you too hard, you know.'

'Not anymore he doesn't,' Lauren said gloomily as they began to walk up the high street together. 'He's just sacked me.'

Elsie stopped so abruptly that Dooley bashed his nose on the back of her leg. 'Sacked you? What do you mean?'

'What do you think I mean? He sacked me. Or, as he put it, he let me go.'

'You're kidding. Why? Not because of

Dooley, surely? Because if that's the case, I'll soon go in and sort him out. If he thinks — '

'No, Elsie. It wasn't about Dooley, although Den wasn't too pleased to find him holed up in his so-called office,' Lauren said as they waited to cross the road at the traffic lights. 'Can you believe it? He actually wants me to go and work for Bradley Northcott. He made it sound like he was doing me this great big favour.'

'Which in a way, Lauren, he is. You're wasted in that place.'

'Now you're sounding like my dad as well,' Lauren said as they turned into Jubilee Terrace, where Elsie lived. 'What is it with everyone today? Has Dad been getting at you?'

'No. But your dad's right. And this could be just the push you need. I don't know why you stayed there as long as you did, to be honest.'

Lauren didn't answer. How could she explain what had kept her at Peas and Cues for all these years? It didn't even make any sense to her, least of all to straight-talking no-nonsense Elsie. But when Lauren started working there as Saturday help while still at school, her mother still ran the craft shop next door; and they'd walk to work together, have lunch together, go home together. And even though the shop was now a mobile phone shop, Lauren still felt that leaving Peas and Cues was one more step away from her mother. A step she wasn't yet ready to take.

But Elsie, as always, wasn't waiting for an answer. Conversation with her was very often a one-way process. 'It's not as if you liked Den Uppington,' she went on. 'But then, who does? Apart from his mother — and even she's always grumbling about his failure to produce a son and heir.'

She was still going on about Den's shortcomings as they stopped outside her little terraced cottage. 'Never trust a man with sandy eyelashes, that's what I always say. And seeing as you're a lady of leisure now, do you want to come in for a cup of tea?'

Lauren shook her head. 'Thanks, but Dad will be home soon and I want to get dinner on. And Scott and I are meeting for a drink this evening. And no, I don't trust Den, Elsie, with or without his sandy eyelashes. But I trust Bradley Northcott even less. There's no way I'm going to work for him.'

★   ★   ★

'I reckon you've got a case for wrongful dismissal there. You could take Den Uppington to the cleaners if you play your cards right,' Scott said later that evening when he and Lauren were sitting in the bar of the Nag's Head. 'And you were quite right to say no to going to work for that Bradley North- cott. He's a dirty old man who can't keep his hands to himself.'

Lauren bit back the urge to tell him to mind his own business. He meant well, but she hated the way he acted as if he was her boyfriend. True, they'd been hanging around together forever. One minute they were part of a big crowd from school; the next, everyone had paired off, most of them married with families now. Except for Lauren and Scott. And everyone, including Scott, assumed they were an item. Even though Lauren always made a point of telling him they were not.

It wasn't that Lauren didn't like Scott. He was a great guy; but his idea of a good night out was footie on the wide screen down the Nag's Head, and his idea of eating out a packet of cheese and onion crisps with a pickled egg popped inside. Furthermore, his idea of how Lauren should spend the rest of her life was a million miles away from hers.

'One of the houses in Jubilee Terrace down the end of your road has just come on the market,' he said, moving his chair around to get a better view of the television screen. 'The old dear's gone in a home and it would be just right for us.'

41

Lauren knew the one he meant. It was two doors down from Elsie's and she'd noticed the For Sale board earlier.

'Right for us?' she echoed, the uncomfortable feeling she was getting in the pit of her stomach having nothing to do with the pickled egg she'd just eaten. 'In what way?'

'You and me. Living together. We've been going out together for four years now. Most women of your age — '

'Your dad's been going on at you again, hasn't he?' Scott's two older sisters were doing their bit to keep the local primary school open by producing seven children between them, all boys. Scott's dad was always dropping hints about Scott and Lauren making up the rest of the football team. He was going to call it 'The Wilde bunch' on account of his surname being Wilde.

'You're not cut out to be a career woman, Lolly,' Scott said with a grin as he peered over her shoulder to see how the football was going. 'What a rubbish pass. Whose side is he meant to be on? Did you see that?'

Lauren shook her head. She was more of a rugby fan herself and not remotely interested in football. One more example of how little she and Scott had in common.

'We can get married, if you'd rather,' Scott said casually as he placed his hand over hers.

Lauren pulled her hand away and said as gently as she could, 'I can't marry you, Scott. You know that. I've told you many, many times. We're good mates, you and me. But that's all we'll ever be.'

That, at least, got his full attention. He looked at her intently without speaking for a long moment. Then: 'This is about leaving your dad, isn't it?' There was an edge of anger in his voice. 'Our mum was only saying yesterday that it's been two years now since your mum passed on. He should have — '

'Stop right there,' Lauren cut in sharply. One part of her wanted to scream at him, but the other more sensible part didn't want everyone in the crowded bar to listen in, which they undoubtedly would. 'I don't want to hear what your mum said,' she hissed. 'Got it?'

Scott was a good mate, but there were two things he did that drove Lauren crazy. The first was when he called her Lolly. But the second — and this was by far the most annoying — was the way he would discuss something she'd told him in confidence with his mum. Sandra Wilde, who had a hairdressing salon in the high street two doors down from Peas and Cues, was that hot at spreading gossip, she was the only person in Stanford who could give Elsie a run for her money.

'It's only because we care about you, babe,' he muttered, taking a long pull at his beer.

'It's because your mother likes a good gossip, more like it,' Lauren said. 'So here's something for her to broadcast. I'm going to take that job

44

with Bradley Northcott — assuming he offers it to me in the first place.'

Scott stared at her in silence for a moment, then scratched his head and said, 'Same again?' which was his answer to most of life's problems.

Lauren watched him go up to the bar. Why had she just said that? No wonder Scott had looked so surprised. She'd surprised herself, because until then she'd decided against it, knowing she was being manipulated by Dodgy Den into doing something that was probably in his best interests but not necessarily in hers.

But Den was right. It was time she moved on. From Peas and Cues, that was. There was no way she'd leave Stoneford, at least not yet. Not until her dad started singing again. Before his wife's illness, Paul Chapman always used to sing about the place, silly songs, half of which Lauren was convinced he used to make up, although he always swore his father used to sing them to him. Even, he assured her, the one that started 'Where's my other flippin' sock?' But the singing, the silly songs, that all ended when Lou died.

He was also an intensely practical man, and Lauren had grown up in the certain knowledge that there was nothing broken that her dad couldn't fix. But not being able to fix his wife's illness had crushed him. He stopped singing. Sometimes, too, Lauren would catch him wandering around the house like a little lost bird. It broke her heart.

But contrary to what Scott expected, she had no intention of staying in Stoneford for the rest of her life. She'd be moving on the minute her dad started singing again. She'd tried explaining that to Scott, but he'd just said she'd feel better after a game of darts and a pint.

She had to do something about Scott. She'd tried several times to explain that they were just mates; that the relationship, such as it was, was never going anywhere. But she hated hurting people's feelings. And Scott's feelings, as he told her, went deep. Although Lauren couldn't help thinking if that was the case, why then did he spend so much time chatting up Keri, the landlord's flame-haired daughter, as he was doing right at that moment?

'Hello again.'

She looked up, and her heart did a ridiculous somersault at the sound of the soft Irish accent. 'I hope you managed to retrieve all your belongings this afternoon and didn't pelt any more white van drivers with tomatoes?' he said with a smile that softened his eyes and lit up his face.

'Word of my accuracy with a tomato must have got around the white van community,' she said, 'because there were no more incidents.'

'I'm sorry I had to rush off this afternoon,' he said. 'I'd just popped out for five minutes without telling the boss. Otherwise I'd have stayed and helped you out.'

'Oh. Thanks.' Lauren was about to ask him where he was working when

Scott came back and put a possessive arm around her shoulder.

'Here you are, sweetheart. Your favourite wine. Dry and white, just as you like it.'

The man stepped away, said, 'Nice to meet you again,' and made his way across to the bar, where Keri nearly cracked her dad's ribs as she elbowed him out of the way, determined to be the one to serve him. Her smile was broad and flirtatious.

'Who was that?' Scott demanded, scowling in his direction.

Lauren shrugged. 'Just someone I almost bumped into this afternoon. I've never met him before. He seemed OK though.'

'Looks a bit on the poncy side if you ask me,' Scott said. 'Linen shirts. I mean, what sort of man wears linen shirts?'

Good-looking Irish ones who could turn a woman's knees to water, Lauren could have said, but didn't. She was really, really going to have to do something about Scott.

'Now, about that job, Lolly,' he began. 'I've been thinking what you said about taking it, and I really don't want you working for Bradley Northcott. The man's a total sleazeball.'

She couldn't disagree with that. Nevertheless, she didn't like Scott telling her what she should and shouldn't be doing. 'I'm sorry,' she said, 'but I don't want to talk about it. Look, I'm afraid I've got a headache coming on. It's been a hell of a day, and I'm going to go home and get an early night.'

'But the football's kicking off any minute,' he said, pointing to the big screen on the other side of the bar.

'It's OK. You stay here and watch it. I'll see myself home,' she said, glad to escape. Glad, too, to get away from the sight of Keri ogling the handsome newcomer — and the sight of him ogling her back.

'No, I'll walk you home. Just be quick about it. I don't want to miss the kickoff.'

'Scott. I don't need . . . ' He drank his pint quickly and gestured for her to do the same. Scott's chivalry, it seemed, would only go so far.

4

'Haven't seen you in here before,' the redhead behind the bar said as she handed Conor his pint. 'You down here on holiday?'

He shook his head. 'No. I'm working here. For a while at least.'

'Oh really?' Conor could tell by the rise of her eyebrows that she was waiting for him to say where. But he was not ready to do that. Yet.

He nodded, smiled and found a seat at the end of the bar, where he took a long pull at his pint. He didn't usually drink in the week, particularly not on this job. He needed to keep his mind fresh and alert. But rules were made to be broken. And after the day he'd had, he needed something. Anything rather than go back to that guest house and be quizzed by the nosiest landlady he had ever met in his life. He thought some of his mother's friends back in Ireland knew how to give a fellow the third degree, but Mrs. Thomson was something else. She'd got half his life history in the five minutes it took to serve him his first breakfast, and if Conor wasn't careful, she'd get the other half before you could say, 'Do you want your eggs fried or scrambled?'

He'd move to a hotel if he could afford it, but splitting up with Helen had proved more expensive than he'd anticipated, and the drop in money between London wages and a small market town in rural Somerset was threatening to become a problem.

The bar was beginning to fill up as people came in to watch a football match that was obviously being broadcast on the big screen that dominated the other end of the bar. Football wasn't his thing. He preferred rugby, but it was a way of whiling away a couple of hours, so he settled down to watch.

He looked across the now crowded bar and saw that the blonde he'd spoken to on his way in was getting up to go. She was obviously not into football either. He felt a twinge of disappointment at that. She was easy on the eye and he was enjoying the view. Until, that was, her boyfriend went with her, his arm draped around her shoulder.

What am I doing? he asked himself. First, breaking his rule about drinking after work, and now chatting up the locals — or at least, getting a bit moody because she was spoken for. Just as well she was, really. She reminded him more than a little of Helen. And look where that had got him. Women were trouble with a capital T, he decided. And he had trouble enough without going looking for more.

His phone pinged with a text message. He read it with a grim smile. Talking of trouble . . . *Any news?* it read. *Why haven't you called?*

He shook his head. Sure, that woman had the tenacity of a terrier at a rabbit hole. *No news*, he texted back. *Call u later*.

He looked down at his glass, surprised to see it was empty. The red-haired barmaid was stacking glasses and smiled as he approached. 'Same again?' she asked, tossing her mane of hair back, her eyes gleaming like they were enjoying what she was seeing.

'Yes, please.' He sat on one of the bar stools and leaned towards her. 'Nice place, this,' he said. 'Lively.'

'It is when the football's on. It can be a bit dead otherwise, like the rest of the town.' She pulled a face.

'It seems a nice town to me,' he said. 'Lots of interesting old buildings.'

'Really?' She looked surprised. 'I can't say I'd noticed. You an architect or something?'

He shook his head. 'Nothing so interesting. I came across this lovely old building on my way here. Sort of tucked away behind a terrace of houses. Looks sadly neglected, though.'

'That'll be the old Founders School building. It's been empty forever. There was talk at one time about it being

54

turned into a community centre — art gallery, café, that sort of thing. But then the woman who was the driving force behind it got sick and died, and no one else wanted to take it on. So like everything else in this place, it never really got off the ground.'

'That's a pity. It's sad to see a lovely old building going to rack and ruin. And the community centre idea seemed like the sort of place that would go well around here.'

She shrugged. 'I doubt it. It's always been like this. Someone gets an idea, says let's do this, and everyone else goes yeah, great, let's go for it. Only when it comes down to it, nobody actually wants to do anything about it. Seen it with the youth club, the football club, you name it. After the first rush of enthusiasm, it just fades away, and nobody wants to know anymore.'

'So who owns that Founders School building?' Conor steered the conversation back in the direction he wanted it to go. 'And why have they allowed it to fall into such a state of disrepair?'

'I don't pay you to stand around nattering, Keri!' a voice behind her growled.

'You don't pay me at all, Dad, remember?' Keri shot back, tossing her head and sending her mane of bright auburn curls bouncing as she turned back to Conor. 'See what I mean about this place? They still exploit their children by making them work all hours in terrible conditions and pay them peanuts. He'll be sending me up the chimney or down the coal mine next.'

'I wish. Maybe then I'd get a bit of peace from your incessant yakking. Does my head in,' her father said, then added with a grin at Conor, 'Kids, eh? Who'd have them? You try and help them out and all they give you is a load of grief.'

'It was my fault,' Conor said. 'I kept her talking.'

'I doubt that. Knowing her, you probably couldn't get a word in edgewise.' He gave Conor a good-natured smile, then turned back to his daughter. 'Look, love, there's a couple of guys down the other end of the bar who look as if they're about to die of thirst. And it's not good for trade to have the customers pegging out in the bar. Passing out's one thing, but pegging out quite another.'

Conor finished the last of his pint and got up to go. As he did, his phone began to ring. He sighed. Talk about people with the tenacity of a terrier at a rabbit hole. If he didn't answer it, he'd get no peace, even though he had nothing to tell her. Although he was beginning to get an inkling.

But he'd wait until he was in no danger of being overheard before taking the call.

*   *   *

'What are you doing up at this time, Izzy?' Bradley asked as Isobel came into the kitchen.

She steeled herself not to respond to the name 'Izzy' even though she knew full well he was not using the contraction of her name as a term of affection, but because she had once in a moment of weakness told him that it was what her mother used to call her and how much she hated it. He'd been using it to wind her up ever since. *But not today*, she decided. *Nothing can wind me up today, not even that.*

Izzy. Such an ugly, ugly word. Now Antonio, he always called her 'Isabella', with the accent on 'Bella'. Which, as everyone knew, meant 'beautiful'. Her insides softened at the thought.

'I was awake early, that's all.' She gave him her brightest smile. 'So I thought I might as well get up. I've got loads to do today.'

He was sitting at the kitchen table, where he'd laid out breakfast for one, as neatly and carefully as if he was serving up a four-course dinner. Matching crockery, a crisp white napkin tucked into his shirt collar, toast in a toast rack — even the marmalade was decanted from the jar into a small serving dish.

Matching, of course. He stopped just short of a twee little vase of flowers in the middle.

When she first met him, she'd thought his attention to detail was quite amusing. Now she simply found it annoying, like almost everything else he did.

'Are you going to eat that last piece of toast?' she asked as she collected a plate and mug (she deliberately chose non-matching ones as she knew it would annoy him) and sat down opposite him.

'Of course.' He spoke without looking up, his attention focused on spreading the butter evenly across the toast. 'Otherwise I wouldn't have toasted two slices of bread, would I?'

And that was another thing about him that annoyed the hell out of her, she thought as her resolve not to let him spoil her sunny mood wobbled. He talked to her as if she was a not-very-bright five-year-old. All he had to do was say 'yes I am', for goodness sake. She put two slices of bread in the toaster and rammed the handle down hard, giving a little smile as she saw him wince.

'So what are you doing today that's so important it has you up at the crack of dawn?' he asked.

For one crazy moment, she was tempted to tell him. *I'm going to meet the love of my life*, she wanted to say. *Someone young and handsome, who doesn't look at me like I'm something unpleasant stuck to the bottom of his shoe. Or treat me like a halfwit.*

If only she could say that. If only she could tell him she wanted a divorce. But if she did that, he'd make sure she didn't get a penny. Oh, he'd been clever. Very clever, had Bradley. She'd been perfectly capable of earning a living when she first met him. In fact, that was how they had met. She'd been his secretary. But as soon as they married, he persuaded her to give up work.

She hadn't needed to be told twice.

The work was as dull and boring as he was, although to be fair, she didn't think of him as boring back then. She thought him smooth, sophisticated and rich, which just goes to show that you never really get to know someone until you live with them.

He was still rich, of course; but as she learned all too soon, incredibly mean with it. And she certainly didn't believe in the smooth and sophisticated bit any more. No, there was no way she was going to let Bradley divorce her. Not without the financial settlement she had more than earned these last sixteen years. If they'd had children, her financial future would be more secure, but it hadn't happened. And now it was too late for her at least — and he'd never wanted children anyway. The mess would have driven him completely over the edge.

So she was certainly going to need a good financial settlement, because unfortunately life and technology had moved on since she'd given up work, and she hadn't kept her skills — such as they were — up to date. Her days as a secretary were long gone. Besides, even Bradley no longer had one. The last one, a rather plump, plain-looking woman in her fifties, if she remembered right, had left six months ago and he'd never got round to replacing her.

'You didn't tell me you'd taken on someone new in the office.' She sat down opposite him, her knee bumping against the table leg as she did so.

'And if I had,' he said coldly as he straightened the plate that she'd knocked out of alignment. 'Would you have been interested? I wasn't aware that my staffing levels were of any interest to you.'

'They aren't,' she said carelessly and took the last of the marmalade that he'd so carefully spooned into the little glass dish. This really was quite fun, she thought. She must get up and have breakfast with him more often. It annoyed the hell out of him; and there was nothing quite like starting the day with a laugh, was there?

'I saw your new man yesterday afternoon,' she said.

That got his attention. He put his knife down and stared at her. 'You did? Where? And how did you know it was him?'

'He was pointed out to me as he was walking down Stoneford high street. I must say, he's not bad-looking. Should start a few young women's hearts fluttering around here, I wouldn't wonder.'

Bradley scowled and got up to spoon more marmalade into the now empty dish. 'And what were you doing in Stoneford high street? Not exactly your usual haunt. Is the Mercedes in for repairs?' He sat back down and looked across the table at her, his eyes bright with suspicion. 'Don't tell me you've pranged it again.'

'Of course I haven't. If you must know, I was having my hair done.'

He gave a sharp bark of laughter. 'You? Having your hair done in Stoneford? Why? Are you sickening for something? Or have you run up so many debts that you're having to start making stringent economies?' He cut his second piece of toast into four exactly equal squares. 'Well, that's no bad thing, I suppose. I shouldn't complain, should I? I take it, then, I'm going to see a marked reduction on the credit card statement this month when I go through it?'

'In your dreams,' she said quickly. 'If you must know, and I can't for a moment believe you're interested, it was an emergency. Sandra Wilde fitted me in at the last moment.'

His thin eyebrows rose and his cold eyes glinted behind his gold-rimmed glasses as he looked at her closely for a moment. 'You're right, I'm not interested. Except to say I can't for the life of me see what she's done. Your hair looks the same as always.'

That's the whole point, she thought. *You can't see I've had my roots done, and nor, I hope, will Antonio.* At the thought of him, her flash of irritation

64

vanished and her sunny mood returned. 'Well, I'm glad you've got someone to help out.'

He scowled but didn't answer.

'Maybe now we could spend a bit more time together.' She knew full well he'd hate the idea as much as she did and did it just to see the look of horror on his face. 'We could maybe go up to London for a few days. See some shows, things like that.'

'Conor's not that much of a help,' he growled. 'He needs constant supervision. He's one of these smart London-trained guys who think they know it all. But, of course, they don't. His way might work fine in the big city, but he's no idea how things operate in a small country town.'

'London-trained?' Isobel's expensively shaped eyebrows raised in surprise. 'Do you mean he's qualified? You've taken on another partner?'

'Hardly.' His thin cold smile never reached his eyes. 'But there's no harm in letting him believe the appointment will lead to a partnership in time, is there? Not that it will, of course. As I said, he really doesn't fit in here. But believing there's the chance of a partnership in the offing keeps him on his toes. Besides, there's something not quite right about him. His story about how he came to be here in Stoneford in the first place is very vague and doesn't make a lot of sense. As a matter of fact, I don't trust the fellow further than I can see him. He's always ferreting around, asking questions and poking his nose into stuff that doesn't concern him.'

'Really?' Isobel wasn't interested in office politics apart from a flicker of worry of the thought of Bradley maybe taking on another younger, prettier woman who might play up to him — the way she had, all those years ago. 'So you're not replacing Mrs Whatever her name was?'

'Mary Jenkins? As a matter of fact, I am. Or I may be. I'm interviewing someone this morning. I'm not sure she's exactly up to the job, but it's only a short-term thing.' He pressed his napkin to his mouth, then folded in neatly in its original folds. 'I've got a few bits and pieces that need sorting out. But I don't need a secretary permanently these days. I've found I've managed perfectly well without one, especially now Conor's around to hold the fort when necessary. In fact, I said to him only yesterday morning . . . '

But Isobel was no longer listening. She looked up at the kitchen clock and her heart gave a leap of excitement — she'd be seeing Antonio in exactly three hours' time. Only one hundred and eighty more minutes!

'Are you playing golf this afternoon?' she asked as Bradley put on his suit jacket, smoothed out imaginary creases and picked up his briefcase with the discreet Mulberry logo stamped on the soft tan leather.

'Of course,' he said. 'It's Wednesday.'

So she was to be a golfing widow once again. Fair enough. She was used to it. But one day, she thought dreamily as she bit into the last piece of toast and scattered crumbs across the table, one day . . .

5

The highly polished brass plaque gleamed golden in the early-morning sun. It read, *Northcott and Company, Chartered Accountants*. A smaller sign below it said, *Please enter*.

Lauren paused and reached up to check her neckline. Not that she needed to, because knowing Bradley Northcott's tendency to leer, she'd chosen a button-to-the neck blue silk blouse to go with the pencil-slim grey skirt she'd decided on for the interview. Not that she was desperate to get the job, as she'd told her father that morning when he'd commented on her changed appearance. She was, she assured him, just going along out of curiosity. But that didn't stop her wanting to make a good impression, to show that she didn't always wear a tabard with *I Mind My Peas and Cues* emblazoned across it.

'Well, I think he'd be bonkers not to hire you on the spot,' her father said as he hugged her. 'You really look the part. Smart, intelligent and businesslike. You know, you really should wear a skirt more often, sweetheart. It suits you.'

Smart, intelligent and businesslike? Yeah right. Her dad, of course, was biased. She was by choice strictly a jeans and T-shirt person, so it felt really weird to be wearing a skirt. And it had taken her so long to find a decent pair of tights that she'd almost made herself late. But she didn't think purple and green striped tights would do much for her 'smart and businesslike' image.

Her long blond hair, which she usually wore in a high ponytail, had taken ages before she was finally able to skewer it into an almost-tidy knot at the nape of her neck. Although she had a horrible feeling that before the day was over, she was going to forget about it and think that something big and hairy had just landed on the back of her neck.

Bradley's office was in an old Victorian building, one of a terrace, and had, she assumed, at one time been a private house. The heavy front door with its ornate fanlight was slightly open. She smoothed back her already smoothed hair, straightened her already straightened skirt, and pushed it open further. Before her was a narrow, gloomy hallway lit only by the light from the fanlight and a small bare bulb. Straight ahead was a narrow staircase, while to her left was a door marked *Reception*.

She knocked and went in. But the room was empty apart from a desk littered with papers, a man's suit jacket hung over the back of the chair, and an out-of-date calendar advertising heating oil. Two spindly-looking chairs made up what was obviously the clients' waiting area over by the bay window that looked out onto the street. She hoped the clients didn't have to wait too long, as the chairs looked as comfortable as concrete blocks, although probably not quite as stable.

Her nose twitched at the smell of musty books and ancient dust that permeated the air. This place could do with what Elsie would call a good old blast of fresh air. It looked as if the windows hadn't been opened in decades.

She checked her watch. In spite of the panic over suitable tights, she was actually a bit early. It was only twenty-five past nine, though the clock on the wall said half past six.

What a dreary place, she thought. It was obvious Bradley Northcott didn't spend his money on flashy offices. No state-of-the-art technology here. As for that old adding machine, the last time she'd seen one like that had been on a school trip to the local museum.

She stiffened at the sound voices in the room above, one of which she recognised as Bradley's. Uncertain what to do, she went out into the dingy hall again but hesitated to go upstairs, because whatever they were talking about, it was certainly not a friendly discussion about last night's football or where to go for lunch. In fact, Bradley sounded furious.

'Of course it was your bloody mistake, man.' His angry voice carried quite clearly to the hall below. 'You smart-ass London guys think you know it all. But when you've had as much experience as I have, you'll learn not to make such an obvious schoolboy error.'

'Schoolboy error, is it?' The other voice, which was vaguely familiar, was equally angry. 'I've been fixing your so called 'schoolboy errors' for the last two weeks. I warned you the Revenue wouldn't accept this. In fact, I said — '

'That's enough, Conor.' Lauren took a step backwards as Bradley's voice rose several decibels. 'You're going the right way to getting fired.'

'Do that and I'll sue you for wrongful dismissal. And while we're thinking about all things legal, you should know that I happened to come across a file this morning that must have fallen down the back of the cabinet. It was for a company called Stag Holdings, so I thought I'd better check it out to see if

73

there were any outstanding queries that needed dealing with. And it made for interesting reading. Very interesting indeed.'

'Stag Holdings? Fallen down the back of the filing cabinet? Of course it hadn't, man. You've been snooping through my private files, haven't you?'

'Private? Oh I don't think so. Not when I read the list of company directors — '

'You had no right — ' Bradley cut in but Conor ignored him.

'Let's put it this way. I don't think the Institute of Chartered Accountants would be too happy about your part in all this, do you?'

There was one of those abrupt silences that reminded Lauren of the day on the school bus when a so-called mate had dared her to say a rude word. And Lauren, never being one to pass on a dare, had said it, unaware of just how very rude the word was until she saw the shocked faces of every adult on the bus. It was the same sort of *did they really say that?* silence. She held her breath and listened.

'Are you by any chance threatening me?' Bradley said in that breathy, uptight way people have of talking when they're only just managing to hang on to their temper. 'Because I really, really wouldn't advise it, young man. You don't know what you're up against here. Now I strongly recommend that you forget about Stag Holdings, go back to your desk and get on with doing what I pay you to do before one of us says something we may later regret.'

Lauren jumped back as the door crashed open and a tall dark-haired man stood at the top of the stairs, his face flushed, his eyes hot and angry. He obviously didn't recognise her, but she recognised him all right. The man Bradley had called Conor was her tomato-rescuing hero of a few days ago, the Benedict Cumberbatch lookalike with the soft Irish accent. Although it hadn't sounded so soft during the exchange with Bradley.

'I'm so sorry, I didn't hear you come in.' He came down the stairs towards her, obviously making a huge effort to speak normally. 'Can I help you now?'

'I hope so.' Lauren flashed him her best smile. 'I'm here to see Mr Northcott. About a job interview. He said to come at half past nine.'

'Right on time.' He glanced up at the clock on the wall that still said half past six, then reached for the phone on the desk. 'I'll tell him you're here. Who shall I say, please?'

'It's Lauren,' she said. 'Lauren Chapman.'

His hand stilled on the phone. He stared at her for a long moment without speaking. Lauren flushed and began to worry she'd got spinach stuck on her teeth, which would have been weird as she didn't make a habit of eating spinach for breakfast. So maybe she'd grown an extra head or two.

'Would that be Lauren Edith Chapman?' he asked in a voice that could have frozen boiling oil.

Lauren lifted her chin and met his cold stare with an equally cool one of her own. Whatever it was that had upset him was nothing to do with her, unless of course he had a violent objection to her middle name. She wasn't overly fond of it herself, to be honest, but as she'd been named after her mother's much-loved grandmother, she put up with it.

'It is,' she said, matching her tone to his.

'Then you'd better go on up, Ms Chapman,' he said. 'He's obviously expecting you. It's the room on the left at the top of the stairs. But then you probably already know that, don't you?'

He looked down at his desk, obviously anxious to get on with his work. She looked at his bent head for a moment, wondering what on earth had just happened. Talk about mean and moody. That man could give Benedict Cumberbatch some lessons.

She smoothed her already smooth

hair, straightened her already straightened skirt and checked her neckline again. She was as ready as she'd ever be to meet Bradley Northcott, who, she sincerely hoped, would be in a better mood than his colleague.

* * *

Bradley's office came as a shock after the dinginess of the reception area. It was thickly carpeted. Floor-length velvet curtains in a rich dark blue hung at the window, while the opposite wall was completely covered by a large glass-fronted bookcase. Oil paintings of sea scenes in gilded frames graced the other walls. But dominating everything was a highly polished desk with a green leather top, the edges of which were embossed with fancy gold patterns. It was the biggest desk Lauren had ever seen and would, she reckoned, have completely filled the small shabby reception room below. It was positioned so that it looked out across the rear gardens to the edge of the town park beyond. A lovely view, no doubt, although it meant that when Bradley was seated at his desk, as he was now, he had his back to anyone entering his office.

He was so deeply engrossed in a file spread out in front of him he was unaware of her presence in the doorway. Lauren was glad she'd taken the trouble to dress smartly. Bradley, as always, was immaculately turned out. He was a small neat man with a small neat head topped with thinning hair brushed neatly back and shiny gold-rimmed spectacles. He wore, as always, a dark well-cut suit, a shirt so white it hurt your eyes, and a tie that obviously proclaimed to those who needed to know that he was a member of a very expensive, very exclusive club.

Lauren cleared her throat and gave a quiet tap on the door to get his attention. Visibily startled, he snapped the file shut and swivelled his chair around.

'Lauren.' He looked surprised to see her.

'The man downstairs said to come on

up. And — and you said half past nine when we spoke on the phone,' Lauren said, cross with herself for sounding nervous.

'Half past nine? Good Lord, is that it time already?' He seemed distracted and not his usual annoying self at all, which was a relief. 'Come along in and take a seat. Shut the door first, though, please, would you?'

As interviews went, it was a weird one. Not that Lauren had had many interviews to measure them by. Bradley muttered something about how she would be working in Reception downstairs; that all she'd have to do was answer the phone, make the tea and do a bit of clerical work.

'I'm used to that,' she said. 'I do most of Den's book-keeping for him, plus his VAT returns, and I'm a quick learner.'

He didn't look as impressed by that as Lauren had hoped, because he then went on to get a bit technical, muttering about debits, credits and bank reconciliations, and did she know

80

what a trial balance was? She'd convinced herself by then that she'd blown the whole thing, so she did what she often did when she was nervous, she cracked a joke. 'Is it some sort of newfangled weighing machine?'

He gave a shout of laughter, sounding much more like his old braying self. 'Den always says you're as sharp as a knife,' he commented as he looked down at her pathetically short CV. 'Yes, I think you'll do well, Ms Lauren E. Chapman. You'll do very well indeed. What does the E. stand for, by the way?'

'Edith,' she said. 'I'm named after — '

'Can you start tomorrow?' he cut in as he picked up the file he'd been reading so intently when she'd come in and began leafing through it.

'Yes, of course,' she said. Feeling herself dismissed, she turned towards the door.

'And don't worry about Den,' Bradley said without looking up. 'I'll sort it with him.'

Lauren hadn't been worrying about

Den and had no intention of working out her notice, not after the high-handed way he'd treated her. She left Bradley's sumptuous office in a bit of a daze. Somehow within the space of a few days she had, as Den had so succinctly put it the day before, gone from cooking apples to cooking the books.

She waited until her father came home from work before telling him about her career change.

'That's great news, chicken.' He looked as pleased as she'd thought he would. 'You were wasted in that greengrocer's shop, and I've never liked that Den Uppington, although your mother always said he was a good guy underneath it all. But then, she could never see the bad in anyone, could she? He's far too up himself for my liking.'

Lauren grinned. 'Did you just make a joke, Dad?' she asked, her heart lifting a little. He'd be singing next.

'Did I?' He looked surprised.

'Uppington. Up himself? It's what Elsie calls him. Councillor Up-Himself.'

'Elsie would,' he said with a smile. 'The older she gets, the more outrageous she becomes. But tell me more about this new job. Northcott and Company, Chartered Accountants. It all sounds very grand, doesn't it?'

Lauren didn't have the heart to prick his happy balloon by telling him that the 'and Company' bit of Northcott and Company consisted of her, a mean moody Irishman called Conor, and an old adding machine that had probably been used by Noah to count the animals in and out of the ark.

But in spite of that, there was a part of her that was looking forward to tomorrow. Maybe Den had done her a favour after all.

6

The row with Bradley that morning had shaken Conor more than he cared to admit. For a moment back there, it was like a mask had slipped, and Conor felt he was looking at the real Bradley Northcott and not liking what he saw very much. And his face when Conor had threatened to report him to the Institute . . . Until that moment, he'd always thought the saying 'if looks could kill, he'd be dead by now' was a bit of a meaningless cliché. Cliché it might be, but in Bradley's case, it was far from meaningless. From the barely controlled body language, Conor had got the feeling that it was more than the sack he was being threatened with.

And then when that woman turned up, the one he'd seen in the high street yesterday afternoon and realised that she was none other than L. E.

Chapman, his mood went from bad to worse. She'd said she'd come about a job interview. What grubby little scheme were they hatching between them? he wondered. No doubt he'd find out if he kept digging. Or had she been brought in to stop him doing just that?

So when later that morning Bradley, his voice icy, suggested that Conor take some papers that needed signatures up to their clients at Stoneford Manor Country Club on the outskirts of the town, Conor for once was happy to go. Normally he'd complain bitterly about being used as an errand boy, but he needed to get away from the office and try and work out what he was going to do next.

He hadn't meant to show his hand quite so soon. But the reaction he'd got when he mentioned Stag Holdings made him think that he was definitely on the right track. If only he'd had time to read and copy that file. The trouble was, Bradley was probably at that moment hiding it, maybe even shredding it, which was why he was so keen to get him out of the office.

Conor drove in through the impressive wrought-iron gates and up a sweeping driveway lined with mature beech trees that led to a large golden stone house cloaked in ivy. For hundreds of years it had been the home of a wealthy local family, until crippling death duties had forced the last of the line to sell it five years ago. Since then it had been converted, at obviously enormous expense, into a sports and leisure club. However, this was no local authority leisure centre, but one of those places where if you had to ask the cost, you probably couldn't afford it.

The house was surrounded by manicured lawns and, discreetly to one side, an outdoor pool and tennis courts. It still had the appearance of a country gentleman's seat until you stepped through the massive oak double doors and into another ultra-modern, uber-expensive world. A world of how the other half lived. Discreet signs pointed to indoor pools, sauna, spa suite and restaurant. The perfect place for the idle rich to idle away a few more hours.

He checked himself. What was the matter with him today? He wasn't usually this judgemental. It was up to people what they did with their money. If he wasn't careful, he'd be turning into an out-and-out socialist, like his grandfather back in Ireland.

As he crossed the silky smooth wooden flooring towards the reception desk, his attention was caught by a couple who'd just come out of what he assumed was the gym and were heading for the restaurant. The man, judging from the logo on his tracksuit top, obviously worked here and was so fit and tanned that Conor found himself wishing he'd kept up his running. The woman had glossy dark brown hair caught back in a high ponytail and reminded him of the way Lauren Chapman had worn her hair the day before. A style which, he reckoned, suited her much better than that severe scraped-back one she was sporting when she'd turned up for her so-called interview this morning.

There was something vaguely familiar about the dark-haired woman, and he was just trying to place her when to his embarrassment she caught him looking at her and came across.

'It's Conor, isn't it?' she said, her smile warm and friendly.

'It is,' he said.

'Don't fret yourself trying to work out who in the blazes I am,' she laughed. 'We haven't met. But I believe you work for my husband. I'm Isobel Northcott.'

She held out her hand. Her nails were long and highly polished in a vivid scarlet shade. And now he was close up, he could see that she was a little older than he'd originally thought. If she'd been working up a sweat in the gym, she certainly didn't show it, although she was dressed in bright pink lycra leggings and a figure-hugging matching top that left little to the imagination.

She was attractive, if a little flamboyant for his taste. He preferred a more natural look on a woman; and once again, without meaning to, his thoughts went back to Lauren Chapman's fresh complexion and clear grey eyes. Who said looks couldn't deceive? he thought sadly.

He brought his attention sharply back to Isobel Northcott. It was hard to imagine this flamboyant, slightly exotic woman with small, neat, ultra-conservative Bradley. 'Pleased to meet you, Mrs Northcott,' he said as she took his hand and held it for a little too long. As she smiled, Conor suddenly realised why he'd thought he recognised her. A photo of her in rather more formal clothes stood on the shelf behind Bradley's desk. Bradley was in a dinner suit, while his wife, who stood a good head taller than him, was wearing a figure-hugging long black dress and some very expensive-looking jewellery. Wherever that picture had been taken, the Northcotts had dressed to impress.

'Isobel, please,' she said. 'And this is Antonio. He's my personal trainer.'

Had Conor imagined it, or was there a significant little pause before the word 'personal'? Certainly the look she flashed the handsome young man was warm and admiring.

'Pleased to meet you, Antonio,' Conor said politely.

'Antonio has the daunting task of getting me fit,' Isobel went on. 'He's quite a cruel taskmaster, you know. Has me almost begging for mercy.' She turned to the younger man. 'Don't you?'

'I try very hard. I am still learning English,' he said. It was obvious from the puzzled expression on his face that he was not fully following the conversation. 'Excuse. One moment please. I have to see — ' He gestured towards the reception desk and went across to it, his movements sleek and powerful. She watched him for a moment, then turned back to Conor.

'So what brings you here, Conor?' she asked. 'Have you come to try out

90

the facilities? They're quite excellent — and the restaurant is fantastic.'

He shook his head. 'Nothing so exciting, I'm afraid. I'm here to get the owners' signatures on a couple of documents.'

'And it gets you out of the office for a while, doesn't it? So why not have lunch while you're here? I'll sign you in.'

Conor shook his head. 'Thanks, but I have to get back.'

She shrugged. 'OK, if you're sure I can't tempt you.' Another flirty little smile, but this time directed at him.

'I'm sorry. These papers are urgent.'

She gave a little pout, which turned to a smile as Antonio rejoined them. 'Fair enough. Now if you'll excuse us, Antonio's promised to introduce me to the delights of wheatgrass and pumpkin-seed smoothies. Personally, I'd prefer a large glass of crisp chilled Vinho Verde, but he's the boss. But maybe later, eh, Antonio? Anyway, nice to have met you, Conor. I'm sure we'll bump into each other again.'

'I hope so, Mrs Northcott,' he said.

'It's Isobel, please,' she said as she laid a hand on Antonio's arm and steered him towards the bar. Conor watched them go, still puzzled by the unlikely pairing of the exuberant, slightly over-the-top Isobel and the buttoned-up, obsessively neat Bradley.

★ ★ ★

The documents signed, Conor got back in his car and, with some reluctance, returned to the office. Bradley was in Reception when he got back, waiting for him. Conor braced himself for another onslaught, but Bradley had obviously used the time Conor was out of the office to calm down.

'Ah Conor, so you found the place all right, did you?' he said, acting as if the row they'd had earlier had never happened.

'All duly signed,' Conor said. 'I'll put them with the accounts and get them sent off to the Revenue with a grovelling letter, and hopefully they'll let it go without slapping a penalty on us for late filing.'

Bradley looked totally unconcerned. 'Don't worry about it. It wouldn't matter if they did. We'd pass it on to the client anyway. They can afford it. So what did you think of Stoneford Manor? It's quite some place, isn't it?'

'Somebody's put an awful lot of money into it.'

'Money that will be returned several times over. Take my word for it, that place is a potential gold mine. There's a waiting list for membership, you know. I always said a good country club was just what this area needed, and I was right. I helped set up the original purchase of the property, you know.' His chest was puffed out like an over-excited pigeon's, and he was obviously expecting a response from Conor. Anxious to keep things sweet between them, for now at least, Conor went along with it and looked suitably impressed.

'It's certainly a grand place,' he said.

'Isn't it just? Thanks to me. You see, that's how it works around here. A few favours called in here and there, and I was able to put them in touch with a property developer who got them a really good deal. That's one of the benefits of living in a small place. It's as much about who you know as what you know. That and keeping your nose to the ground and your ears open, of course. That way, you get to hear things. Sometimes, you know, you're better off being the big fish in the little pond.'

'Yes, I'm beginning to see that,' Conor murmured, hoping that now Bradley was back to his usual boastful self-important self, he might be led on to reveal even more. 'You've obviously got an eye for a good deal.'

Bradley smirked. 'I happened to know that the family were in all sorts of financial problems with death duties and inheritance tax, so the developers were able to get the place at a knock-down price as the family were desperate to sell.' His small pale eyes gleamed behind his gold-rimmed glasses. 'As a result, my wife and I have free membership for life. That's what I call a win/win situation. Not bad, eh?'

'Not bad at all. Like I said, it looked a very nice place. And busy too.'

'It's nice enough. I prefer the golf club. But my wife likes it and seems to spend half her life there.'

And I think I can see why, Conor could have added, but didn't. He needed to keep the peace between him and Bradley for just a little longer. 'And I suppose that's how you got involved with that other property company . . . what was it called? Stag Holdings? Was that another of your win/win situations?'

Bradley stiffened. 'What is it with you? Why are you so interested in that? The company's not even active anymore. The file should have been put in the archives months ago, but since Margaret left, the routine office work has slipped a bit I'm afraid. As a matter of fact, I've got it here. You're welcome to have a look at it. As you'll see, it's all aboveboard.'

He handed Conor the file. It was all a little too easy for Conor's liking. Earlier, Bradley had gone to great lengths to prevent him seeing it. Conor was prepared to bet that it hadn't ended up behind the filing cabinets by mistake. And yet now, here he was handing it over. Conor was pretty sure that when he looked inside, there would be very little to help him. Bradley had obviously made the most of Conor's absence from the office and done a little judicious 'filing' of his own.

'Thanks.' The moment Conor took the file, his suspicions were realised. It was considerably thinner than it had been the last time he'd seen it, and he cursed the fact that he hadn't had enough time to look through it properly. All he'd seen was the list of shareholders — and the name L. E. Chapman right at the top of that list.

'The woman who came this morning,' he said, keeping his voice as casual as he could, 'she said it was for an interview. Is that right?'

Bradley nodded. 'Lauren. Yes, I think she'll do OK. Like I said, I've had to let the routine office work slide a bit since Margaret left, and it's a waste of your time and ability to do it. Lauren's a bright woman, even if she's a little too sure of herself sometimes for my liking.' He paused. 'I've known her forever. Lost her mum a couple of years ago and it shows. Her father lets her have her own way far too much, and she can be a bit of a wild child at times. But like I said, she's bright enough, and eager to learn.'

'And you'd like me to show her the ropes, would you?'

'No, no. Again, that would be a waste of your time and talents,' Bradley said smoothly. 'No, you carry on working your way through that client list I gave you. I'll see to Lauren.' He gave a sudden not-very-pleasant smile that reminded Conor of a crocodile in a picture book he used to have as a child.

'She'll be safe enough in my hands, I can assure you.'

Conor wasn't convinced about that. Judging from the little he'd seen of Lauren Chapman, he reckoned the woman was more than capable of taking care of herself.

7

Isobel still had her hand on Antonio's arm as they walked into the bar. She could feel the taut muscles flexing as they moved, and it set her fingers tingling to their very tips. Added to which, she revelled in how good it felt to be walking with a man who was a little taller than her. She'd always been conscious of her height and hated the fact that Bradley was several inches shorter than her. Then there was his thinning hair, which he made look even thinner by insisting on sleeking it back with some sort of horrible-smelling gel that he plastered on it. When they were first married, she'd tried to convince him that it would look a lot better with a smart cut and without the gel, but he wouldn't be told. And she'd stopped caring about how he looked now.

Antonio's hair, by contrast, was thick

and as black as a raven's wing, and when he bent forward, a lock of it would fall over one eye, making her long to reach out and brush it back. She could just imagine what it would feel like to trail her hands through his hair, to see those lovely dark chocolate eyes soften at her touch. Her breathing quickened, and her heart began to race as if she was still on that wretched treadmill.

They walked across to a table that overlooked the manicured lawns and carefully sculpted shrubs. He pulled out a chair for her.

'You sit. I bring,' he said with a dazzling smile.

'Thank you.' She was almost purring as she sat. Such lovely manners. When was the last time Bradley held a chair out for her? Or smiled at her in a way that made her feel the most beautiful, desirable woman in the world? Never.

When she'd first met him, she'd been dazzled by his wealth. But she knew Antonio wasn't wealthy. He wouldn't be working in this place if he was. But it didn't matter. Which surprised her, because if she were ever to be asked, she'd say that wealth was the most important thing she looked for in a man, and made no secret of the fact that it was just that that had attracted her to Bradley. But the fact that she wasn't bothered that Antonio didn't have any money could only mean that she was in love with him, because she'd never felt like that about a man before.

'Here, Isabella,' he said in that lovely soft voice that made her toes curl. 'You drink. Very good. No?'

She took a sip. It tasted foul, a cross between lawn clippings and rotting seaweed. Not that she'd ever tasted either. But if she had, it would probably have tasted like this. But he was looking at her so anxiously, so eager to please, that she forced herself to swallow it. And with a supreme effort of will, she forced herself to smile as well.

'Mmm, delicious. It tastes good,' she murmured, anxious not to hurt his feelings.

He looked surprised for a moment then threw his head back and laughed. 'No. No,' he said. 'I don't think it taste good. It taste very bad. But I mean, it is good. Good for you. Lots of vitamins. Good for skin. Make you even more beautiful.'

Beautiful? He really thought she was beautiful? Her cheeks began to glow. 'In that case, I'll drink it,' she said. 'But I promise you, I'm going to have a large gin and tonic chaser to take the taste away when I've done so.'

He shook his head. 'Oh no, no. Not good, drinking alcohol in day. That is bad for skin. I, Antonio, will make you even more beautiful. Toned muscles. Clear skin. You look like new woman if you follow my plan. Here. In paper. All explain better than me.'

He handed her a folder embossed with the country club's crest. It gave details of a series of one-to-one personal training sessions which included weight training and dietary advice, among other things.

'Is twelve weeks. Three times a week.

You and me, OK? You like?'

She liked very much. OK, the cost wasn't covered by her free membership, so Bradley wouldn't like very much. And she'd need to work out a way to pay for it without him finding out, which would not be easy. But who cared, if it was a chance to see Antonio on a one-to-one basis three times a week for the next twelve weeks? It sounded like heaven to her. Apart from the treadmill. And the weight training. And that godawful stepper which nearly killed her. The hour she'd just spent with Antonio in the gym had been sheer torture. But it was worth it. He was worth it.

'I'll give it some thought,' she said.

He looked puzzled again and gave a little shrug of frustration. 'My English,' he said. 'No good. I — I need learn. But expensive. Too expensive.'

'I could teach you.' She leaned towards him, her eyes shining. 'Oh, nothing formal, of course. But conversational English.' Again, she saw his puzzled frown and explained, 'Just sitting, talking. Like we're doing now. But in a more relaxed place. Not here.'

He nodded. 'That would be good.'

'We could start tomorrow, if you're free?' she went on. 'There's a small country pub I know that's very quiet. I could drive you there. We sit and talk for an hour. I drive you back. If — if you like.'

'I like. I like very much.'

'So where are you staying?'

'Here. Staff — ' He paused and pointed to an accommodation block to the rear of the main building.

'Accommodation?' she suggested. 'You sleep there? In that building?'

'*Sim, sim*. I mean, yes, yes. Acc-ommodation?' He stumbled over the syllables. 'Yes?'

'Perfect.' She clapped her hands. 'See? I think we'll do very well, don't you? You're a very bright pupil.'

'And you. Very bright . . . '

'Teacher,' she said.

'Very bright teacher,' he repeated and

gave her a huge beaming smile. It was like the sun had just come out, and Isabel lapped it up.

'I'll see you tomorrow then,' she said as she stood up to go. 'What time?'

'My last client is six o'clock.'

'About half past seven then? Would that be OK?'

'Half past seven. And thank you. And you will think about — ?' He pointed at the folder with the personal training details in it.

'I'll think about it,' she promised. 'We'll talk about it tomorrow, shall we?'

She almost danced her way out of the country club. Signing up for an expensive one-to-one course would have been difficult to get past Bradley's eagle eye. But her offer to teach Antonio English would give her ample time to be alone with him. And Bradley need never know.

Yes, somehow she just knew that he was going to be a very bright pupil. Very bright indeed. And with a bit of luck, there would be more on the curriculum than English. Maybe her homework for today would be to find out how to say 'I love you' in Portuguese.

*   *   *

Lauren held her breath as she crept past Elsie's house. She prayed that Dooley wouldn't be in her favourite spot in the window, ready to bark at her and give her away. She'd only been working for Northcott and Company for six days and she'd been late four times, all of them down to Elsie.

Every time she saw Lauren go past — and it was like she'd been sitting in her window looking out for her, or else she'd primed Dooley to act as lookout — she'd bustle out with something 'important' she had to tell her.

'I'm glad I've caught you, Lauren,' she called out that morning just as Lauren was beginning to think she'd got away with it.

'Actually, Elsie, I'm sorry, but I really am in a bit of a hurry — '

106

'I won't keep you a moment. But I thought you'd want to hear this. I was at my club yesterday afternoon and everyone was saying how much they missed you at Peas and Cues. How things aren't the same without your cheery smile.'

'That's very kind of them, but — '

'And what do you think that swindler Den tried to palm me off with yesterday?'

'Knowing Den, it could be anything from soggy celery to rotting rhubarb,' Lauren said while the wind funnelled down Jubilee Terrace with such ferocity that it turned the road into a wind tunnel and tugged at her hastily pinned-up hair.

'He was only trying to get me to buy some of those auburn jeans. I mean, what would I want them for, for goodness sake?'

What indeed? Elsie was strictly a 'nice comfy pair of slacks with an elasticated waist' sort of person, and Lauren was still trying to picture her strutting her stuff in a pair of auburn jeans when she twigged what she was on about. 'Aubergines, Elsie,' she said, stifling a laugh. 'I think you mean aubergines.'

'Whatever you call them, they're still nasty-looking foreign things,' Elsie sniffed. 'And I told him I didn't want yesterday's squashy tomatoes either, thank you very much.'

'Quite right,' Lauren said as she struggled to hold her hair in place before the wind completely wrecked it. 'Look, I've got to go. I'm going to be late, and — '

But Elsie hadn't finished with her yet. 'So how's the job going?' she asked as Lauren edged away. 'And how's that nice young man?'

'If by nice young man you mean Conor, he's fine.' Lauren thought Elsie probably knew more about him than she did. Over the last week, Elsie had informed her that he was twenty-eight years old, born in a little village just outside Dublin, had lived and worked in London until a few months ago, and was now staying at Bessie Thomson's B&B in Richley Road. Lauren also learnt that he kept himself to himself, didn't care for marmalade, and was nursing a broken heart — which, she thought, maybe explained his grumpiness. Although she was tempted to ask, if he kept himself to himself, how did Mrs T know he was nursing a broken heart? But she let it go, as she knew what Elsie could be like once she got started on Mrs T, her arch-rival in gossip, and she couldn't afford the time. She was already running late. Again.

'The job's fine, too,' she went on quickly before Elsie could start up another line of conversation. 'And I'm sorry about Peas and Cues, I really am. Only I've really, really got to dash. Sorry.'

But even if Lauren hadn't been running late, she probably wouldn't have told Elsie the truth. Which was that, in fact, the job wasn't fine. That it was a million miles from what she'd expected. That all she did was answer the phone, make coffee, run errands, make more coffee. And, just for a change, in the afternoons she'd make tea. The truth was she was just a dogsbody, and a pretty bored one at that.

As for Conor, Elsie's so called 'nice young man', he'd hardly said a civil word after the day of the interview. Now that Lauren was working in Reception downstairs, he spent all his time beavering away in a tiny little office scarcely bigger that Den's cleaning cupboard, at the very top of the building. And even when she trudged all the way up there with his coffee, all she would get was a polite but distant thank-you.

In fact, the whole thing was so bad that Lauren found she actually missed Peas and Cues. And if the customers missed her, then she surely missed them. She missed having a laugh and a chat. She missed watching the world go

110

by outside the shop window and the chaos as the children came out of school. She even missed Den and his rubbish jokes.

'Lauren?' Elsie called her back, her pointy little face puckered in a frown. 'There was something I wanted to say to you. Something serious.'

'What sort of serious? Not more auburn jeans, surely?' Lauren grinned.

But unusually, Elsie didn't return the smile. Instead, she put her hand on Lauren's arm and looked up at her, her sharp bird-like eyes intent. 'You will be careful, lovey, won't you? As you know, I'm not one to spread gossip, but I think you should know that I've heard things. About Bradley Northcott — '

'Oh that!' Lauren squirmed at the prospect of another of Elsie's lectures on how to deal with a man's 'phillydanderings', as she put it. Since her mother's death, Elsie had taken somewhat too keen a personal interest in Lauren's moral welfare. 'He's harmless, honest, Elsie. Besides, I can handle him. I'm a couple of inches taller than him, for a start.'

'I dare say you can 'handle' him, as you put it,' Elsie sniffed. 'But I wouldn't say he's harmless. And he's up to something. You mark my words. He was around here the other day with a man in a suit. Deep in conversation, they were. And they weren't here to admire my forsythia, that's for certain.'

'Well, yes, but — '

'And I'll tell you who else was here that day. That Roger Newton, the shifty-eyed fellow your friend Scott works for. Poking around old Annie Bennett's house. I wouldn't have thought it was his sort of place at all, not with that wife of his. Wouldn't lower herself to live in Jubilee Terrace, that one, in spite of the fact that she used to work on the bacon counter in the Co-op. I remember when she — '

'Do you mean the house that's up for sale?' Lauren cut in quickly. 'Roger Newton was looking around that? Are you sure?'

'Of course I'm sure. There's nothing wrong with my eyesight.' Elsie peered at Lauren. 'What's wrong? You look like you've bitten on a wasp.'

'Nothing's wrong,' Lauren said, but there was a knot of anger coiled in her stomach. 'But if I don't get to work, something will be very wrong. Because I'll get the sack. So I'll catch you later, OK?'

And if she caught Scott later, she'd really let him have it. How dare he have the nerve to get his boss to check out Annie's house, when only last week Lauren had made it perfectly clear to him she'd no intention of living in it with him? What was he playing at?

Scott Wilde suffered from the worst kind of selective deafness. He only ever heard what he wanted to hear. But next time Lauren caught up with him, she'd make sure he heard her loud and clear, even if she had to hit him over the head to do so.

8

Lauren was still planning what she was going to say to Scott when she reached the office, and her mood was not helped by the fact that Conor was in Reception sorting through the morning's post when she came in.

'Good morning,' he said politely enough, but it was the way he looked up at the clock — which was still saying half past six — that annoyed Lauren even further.

'What's the point of having a clock that never shows the right time?' she said crossly.

'Ah, but you're wrong there. It shows the right time twice a day. At half past six in the morning and half past six in the evening. So, it can't be all bad, can it, now?'

His lips twitched in a smile, and for the first time since the tomato-throwing incident, he wasn't looking at her like she was something unpleasant stuck to the bottom of his shoe.

She smiled back. 'Fair point,' she said.

There was a sudden awkward silence, broken only by the hum of traffic on the road outside. They stood staring at each other, as if they were in a film that had suddenly frozen. He reached out a hand and touched a lock of her hair that had been dislodged by the wind. A shock-wave jolted through Lauren's body, like an electric shock but nicer. Much, much nicer.

She didn't want to break the spell by doing anything as mundane as breathing. His eyes, she noticed, which she'd thought were just brown, actually had little flecks of gold in them, while a tiny muscle flickered at the corner of his mouth.

What was going on? She took a step back and as she did so, he did the same.

'You — er — you look like you're about to lose a hair clip,' he said, his voice sounding as if he'd just run up a flight of stairs. Lauren's heart was thudding as if she'd just run up that same flight of stairs after him.

She reached up to repin her hair, but before she could do so, the internal phone buzzed. It was Bradley, demanding coffee. And the moment of madness, whatever it was, was over. Conor gathered up the pile of post and retreated to his little room at the top of the building.

She had recovered her breath — and repinned her hair — by the time she took Bradley's coffee up to him. 'I'd prefer my coffee in the cup, Lauren, if it's all the same to you,' he growled. 'And sit down for a moment, will you? I've been giving the matter of your training programme some thought.'

Training programme? Things could be looking up, after all. First Conor. Now this. She sat down and looked expectantly at him across the vast expanse of his desk. She waited while he opened his desk drawer, took out a box of tissues and carefully wiped up the spilt coffee in the saucer.

'I'm sorry about that,' she said. 'It's that great big stone you use as a door stop. I stubbed my toe on it as I came in, and — '

'Then you'll be more careful next time, won't you?' he cut in as he balled up the used tissue and dropped it in the waste basket.

'I'm really looking forward to getting my teeth into something,' Lauren went on. 'Like I said in my interview, I'm a quick learner. And, well, to tell you the truth, I've been getting a bit bored just answering the phone and making the coffee. I'd really love to get down to some real work.'

He flicked an imaginary fleck of dust off his immaculate desk, then looked at her without speaking for several long minutes. Then he gave a small nod, as if he'd just made up his mind about something. 'Right, then. So how do you fancy becoming a company secretary?' he asked.

The question took her by surprise. 'I'm afraid I don't do shorthand.'

'Not that sort of secretary,' he said with a cold patronising smile that she tried to ignore. 'It's a service we offer our clients, particularly the smaller companies, whereby we deal with all the statutory legal stuff on their behalf. All you have to do as company secretary is sign and seal a few forms, file them with Companies House and that's it. Job done, as I believe you young people would say.'

'But I don't know anything about legal stuff,' Lauren said, her voice full of doubt. 'I'm not sure — '

'For goodness' sake, woman,' he said, his voice crackling with irritation. 'There's nothing to it. I'm not asking you to sign away your life savings. It's just a lot of boring legal rubbish that you won't even have to read, least of all understand.' He looked at the slim gold watch on his wrist. 'I don't have time to go through it now, but how about you come in early tomorrow morning and we'll go through it then. Shall we say 8.15?'

'Of course. I'll be here.' Lauren realised that one of the benefits of coming in early was that she should be able to give Elsie the slip for once.

He started straightening the already perfectly straight pile of papers on his desk, which Lauren took as her signal to leave. But as she got up to go, he called her back.

'One last thing, Lauren. Whatever you do, don't mention this to Conor.'

'Oh?' Lauren thought this wasn't the time to say to Bradley that she and Conor weren't exactly on speaking terms. But she was curious to know why Bradley had said that. 'Why not?'

He steepled his fingers together and sighed. 'Well, if you must know, it's because he doesn't think you're up to the job. So it's best to do it while he's not around. Which is why I've asked you to come in early tomorrow. What the eye doesn't see and all that. Besides,' he added, his eyes glinting behind his gold glasses, 'an early start will make up for the late one you had this morning, not to mention the other three late starts. Punctuality isn't exactly your strong point, Lauren, is it?'

★   ★   ★

'Well?' Lauren demanded when she met Scott in the Nag's Head later that evening. 'Do you have something to tell me?'

Scott looked at her blankly. 'What? Have I missed your birthday or something? Our anniversary?'

Lauren gave an exasperated sigh. 'Scott. There is no 'our' anniversary. I was thinking more about Jubilee Terrace. Were you going to tell me? I thought I said — '

She stopped talking as Keri came up and started clearing glasses. She gave Scott a big beaming smile but ignored Lauren.

'Do you mean you've changed your mind about Jubilee Terrace?' Scott's face lit up and he reached across and grabbed Lauren's hand, almost knocking his glass over as he did so. 'I knew it. I'll ring the agent tomorrow to arrange a viewing, shall I? Perhaps I should get Dad to come along and have a look at it. Looks sound enough to me. But you never know — '

Lauren pulled her hand away and said, once she was sure Keri was out of earshot, 'Why would you need your dad when your boss has already given it the once-over? Don't deny it, Scott. He was seen.'

'But why would I do that?' Scott's tone of injured innocence sounded convincing enough, but Lauren had been caught by it before. Not this time.

'Why wouldn't you?' Lauren said. 'You get a bee in your bonnet about us setting up home together and, without waiting for me to agree to it — which, as I told you yesterday, I never would — you get your boss to go round and check it out for you. Honestly, Scott, sometimes I could — I could — '

'I didn't. I swear on my granny's grave, I didn't ask him anything of the sort.'

'Your granny is alive and well and living it up in Weston-super-Mare,' Lauren said, although she was beginning to think that maybe she'd been a bit hasty in her accusation because he really did look genuinely surprised by the whole thing. 'OK, I'm sorry. I believe you. Your boss was obviously there for some other reason. But forget about getting in touch with the estate agent, OK? There's no way you and I will be moving in together. In Jubilee Terrace or anywhere else. Apart from taking out a full-page ad in the *Stoneford Advertiser*, I really don't know how else to make you understand.'

He drained his pint and put the empty glass on the table. 'OK. OK. I get it. But blimey, Lolly, I'd never have invited you out this evening if I'd known you were going to be in such a foul mood,' he grumbled. 'I must say, working for old Bradley has done nothing for your mood.'

'I'm not in a bad mood,' Lauren snapped. 'And if I am, it's hardly my fault.'

'Job not working out then?' he said with a smug grin that made Lauren want to tip her wine over his head. 'I told you it was wrong for you, didn't I?'

'Yes, well, you also told me England would win the World Cup, so you're not exactly fortune teller of the year, are you?' she said, then grinned. She could never stay cross with Scott for long. 'Oh, forget it. Are you ready for another beer? My round, to say sorry for snapping your head off just now.'

'And that you'd got the wrong end of the stick?'

'Don't push it, Scott Wilde. Do you want another beer or not?'

She said, 'A pint of best and a Pinot Grigio, please, Keri,' as she went up to the bar, and was rewarded with another glare. She and Keri had never exactly been best mates, ever since she'd

123

beaten Keri to the part of Sandy in the school production of *Grease*. And although that was seven, maybe even eight years ago now, Keri, like so many people in Stoneford, had a long memory.

'You and Scott having a lovers' tiff?' she said.

Lauren sighed. 'Hardly. Scott and I are just mates.'

'Not very good mates, by the look of it. I thought for a moment you were going to tip your drink clean over his head.'

'It would have been nothing more than he deserved,' Lauren said as she handed Keri the money and picked up the two glasses.

'I hear you're working for that old lech, Bradley Northcott,' Keri said with a grimace. 'Rather you than me.'

'He's all right. I don't see that much of him, to be honest.'

'And what about that dishy Irishman? Conor, is that his name? Do you see much of him? No? But I bet you'd like to. I must admit, he's quite tasty. I wouldn't mind seeing a bit more of him, in both senses of the word, if you know what I mean.'

Lauren shook her head. 'Not my type,' she said, and tried not to remember that moment in the office this morning when he'd reached out and touched her hair.

'You wish,' Keri was saying. 'But, just so you know, I'm pretty sure he fancies me. I can always tell.' She tossed her long red mane of hair back and gave a knowing smile. 'He's been in here several times in the last few days, asking an awful lot of daft questions, but all of them with a definite twinkle in his eye. I think it was just an excuse to chat me up. Is he married, do you know?'

'No, I don't. You probably know more about him than I do,' Lauren said. 'Well, you and Bessie Thomson.'

'Is that where he's staying? Poor guy.' She pulled a face, then leaned forward, her green eyes gleaming with mischief. 'Hey, is that what you and Scott were rowing about just now? Are you using Conor to make Scott jealous?'

'As if.' Lauren tried not to show her annoyance. Keri always managed to find a way to get under her skin. 'Why would I want to make Scott jealous?'

'Well, you know. I've heard all about these office romances. Bonding over the photocopier, that sort of thing.'

'I hardly ever see him. Or anyone else, come to that,' Lauren said in a burst of honesty. 'If you must know, I spend most of my time filing and making the tea.'

Keri pulled a face. 'Doesn't sound much of a job to me.'

Already Lauren was regretting her earlier honesty. 'It's early days. In fact, I'm starting on a new training programme tomorrow. I'm going to become a company secretary.'

'Sounds totally dullsville to me,' Keri said with a shrug, then turned away to serve someone down the other end of the bar while Lauren went back to Scott. But he'd started a game of darts with one of his mates.

Time, she reckoned, to finish her drink and go. She had to be in work early tomorrow, so an early night beckoned.

9

As Isobel sat outside the staff accommodation block at the country club waiting for Antonio, she couldn't help going over the ugly scene she'd had with Bradley that evening. She was still shaking from it.

She shouldn't have said it, really. It was stupid — and totally untrue. Although Bradley didn't know that. And for a moment back there, she'd really, really thought he was going to hurt her. And if looks could kill, she'd certainly be dead by now.

It had started, like so many of their rows had, about money. For a man as wealthy as Bradley was, he was also incredibly mean, and went through the credit card statement every month with a magnifying glass. This month was no exception.

'The bill from the country club is a

bit hefty this month,' he said, 'considering I don't have to pay for the basic membership. What have you been doing, treating the whole aerobics class to lunch in the restaurant?'

'Of course not.' She flushed. 'If you must know, I had a couple of one-to-one sessions with a personal trainer.'

He gave a bark of laughter but his eyes were as cold and humourless as ever as he looked at her. 'Well, whatever she's doing, I should ask for your money back. You're still as awkward and unco-ordinated as ever. You wouldn't make it past the fourth tee on the golf course. I'm thinking now I'll revoke our membership. I never use the place, and all the extras they stick on the bill each month are beginning to add up.'

Isobel's heart lurched at the thought of no country club, no Antonio. And just when things were going so well between them. 'You — you can't do that,' she protested. 'I — I'm really beginning to feel the benefit of all that exercise. And yes, the one-to-one sessions are expensive, but it's only to start with. Once my programme is in place, I'll be able to do it on my own. Besides, it's still far less than you spend at your precious golf club.'

'Yes, my dear, it probably is. But you're forgetting one thing. Well, several things.' His patronising tone set her teeth on edge. 'Number one, I'm the one who goes out and earns the money to pay all the bills. Unless, of course, you're thinking of re-entering the job market? No?' He gave a smug sneer. 'Thought not. And number two, I do a lot of business on the golf course and, unlike you, am not there to while away a few hours just because I'm bored.'

'I'm not — ' she began, but he cut across.

'And I'm getting rather bored with this conversation every month,' he said. 'In fact, to be perfectly honest, I'm getting bored with you. With our marriage.'

Isobel's heart gave another lurch as the conversation, which had begun badly, suddenly got a whole lot worse. 'What — what do you mean?' she asked, although she had a horrible feeling she knew exactly what he meant.

'I mean divorce. I wouldn't say our marriage is working out, would you? And like I said, I'm getting pretty tired of picking up your bills every month. Face it, Izzy.' His voice softened. and for a moment he looked genuinely sorry. 'I'm a confirmed old bachelor. I should never have got married in the first place.'

'But you're not old — '

'It's not just the age gap between us,' he went on as if she had never spoken. 'It's everything. We're just totally incompatible. I thought you'd perhaps grow into your role as my wife — I do, as you know, have a position of some standing within the community — but sadly, that hasn't happened. I thought you'd host dinner parties, entertain my friends. Be an asset to me. Instead of which . . . ' The shrug of his shoulders said it all.

He was talking like it was already decided, and she felt a wave of panic rise up in her. But not for long. The panic was soon replaced by anger. Sheer blazing anger. The pompous little prat. Grow into the role of his wife? How dare he! She wasn't going to beg, damn him, if that was what he was hoping for.

'I don't think divorce would be a very good move on your part, Bradley,' she said coldly. 'Because you're forgetting one very important thing.'

'Oh? And what would that be?'

'You're forgetting I was your secretary at the time you and your cronies were setting up Stag Holdings. And even an airhead like me — that's what you called me, wasn't it? — even an airhead like me overhears things sometimes and can put two and two together. Divorce? I rather think not. Or, if we do, it would mean a very generous settlement on your part. Remember this, Bradley. A word in the right place and I can bring your grubby little empire crashing down around your ears. I could ruin you. And don't for a moment think that I wouldn't.'

She shouldn't have said that. She really, really shouldn't have said that. For a start, it wasn't true. She didn't really know anything about Bradley's business dealings, even when she was working for him. Except that she'd always remembered how he would react if she came in to his office if he was talking about Stag Holdings. He'd shut up and wait for her to leave, his fingers drumming impatiently on the desk. She also remembered how he kept the files pertaining to it in a locked drawer in his desk. But that was all. And, to be honest, she wasn't that interested. To her it was all boring, and even though she typed all his correspondence, she never really bothered to try and find out what it was all about. Tax appeals and auditors' reports could have been written in Greek — or, come to that, Portuguese — for all she took in.

But Bradley didn't know that. And

she had no intention of telling him. Whatever it was about Stag Holdings, she'd certainly hit a nerve. His face went purple. His eyes bulged in their sockets. For a moment, she thought he might be having a heart attack. But no such luck. Instead, he was literally shaking with anger. Consumed by it. For a moment, she really thought he was going to lash out at her with his fists that were clenched so tightly by his sides his knuckles were white. She took a step backwards, her hip connecting with the corner of the kitchen unit as she did so.

But no, he didn't lash out with his fists. That wasn't his way. His choice of weapon always had been words.

'You stupid, stupid little . . . ' The words poured out of him. Cruel, biting words that cut through her like a knife, undermining her confidence, tearing away at her self-esteem. She should have been used to it. Goodness knew she'd been on the receiving end of his vicious tongue more times than she could remember. But this was particularly vicious, even by his standards.

Even now, an hour later, as she sat here in the car waiting for Antonio, she could still hear the terrible things Bradley had said to her rattling around inside her head. And she knew that tonight when she went to sleep, those words would come back again. Thank goodness she and Bradley had been sleeping in separate rooms for some years now. Her only regret, in fact, was that her bedroom door didn't have a lock on it.

It had ended saying with Bradley saying he was going to start divorce proceedings the very next day and advising her to get herself a lawyer. 'And, of course, a job,' he said. 'Because you're going to need one. I hear the local greengrocer's is looking for a new shop assistant. Shall I put in a word for you with Den Uppington? He owes me a few favours.'

'I don't think so,' she said, playing her part for all she was worth. 'I think you'll find that we can come to a settlement that's to our mutual advantage. Now if you'll excuse me, I've got a meeting to go to. Don't wait up for me, Bradley.'

As exit lines went, it wasn't bad. It would, however, have been totally ruined if he could have seen how much her knees were shaking as she picked up her coat and handbag and went out to her car.

* * *

'I do not like much your English weather,' Antonio said as he got into the car, droplets of rain clinging to his hair. 'Rain. Rain. Always the rain.'

Isobel laughed. Just the sight of him chased away her dark mood. 'And I thought it was only us English who moaned about the weather all the time.'

She started the engine and eased her sleek silver sports car out of the country club and along the narrow lane that led to the quiet country pub she'd chosen as a perfect location for their informal English lesson. The driving rain showed no sign of letting up when they reached the pub.

'Come on, let's make a dash for it,' she said. 'There's no point waiting for it to ease up. We could be here all night.'

A gust of wind almost snatched the car door from her as she went to open it, and by the time they'd hurried across the pub car park, they were both cold and wet.

But inside the pub it was warm and cosy. The bar was empty except for a couple of old men at the other end who were far too engrossed in their game of cards to take any notice of them. A log fire hissed and crackled in the grate, filling the place with the sweet earthy scent of burning wood. Isobel sat down at the table closest to it and reached her hands towards the dancing flames. As she did so, she noticed how the firelight sent ricochets of rainbow-coloured light flashing off the large diamond Bradley had given her when they'd got engaged.

And she made a mental note to pop into a jeweller's and find out how much it was worth. Not in Stoneford of course. The jeweller was one of Bradley's cronies.

She felt the tension of the run in with Bradley drain out of her as she waited for Antonio to come back with the drinks. He placed them — a fizzy water for her and a diet Coke for him — in front of them. He'd collected some leaflets from a cardboard stand that stood on a side table near the bar, advertising local attractions.

'I read this to you, yes?' he asked.

Isobel nodded and he began to read a leaflet extolling the attractions of a nearby farm park.

'Tractor rides. Sheep sh — ' He paused and frowned over the word.

'Shearing. Sheep shearing,' she said, and made a motion with her hands to show a pair of clippers in use. 'The sheep have long wool in the winter, which is cut off in the summer.'

'Yes. I understand.' He nodded and

went back to the leaflet. 'Donkey rides. Cream teas.'

'Perfect.' She smiled. 'But let's find something more interesting to read, shall we? Here, I've got just the thing. Try this.' She took a leaflet out of her bag and handed it to him. It was advertising the local theatre and the latest amateur dramatics club production that was being put on there.

'*A Murder is Announced,*' he read slowly and carefully. 'What is this, please?'

'It's the name of a play. It's being put on at the theatre next week. I'm going to see it. Would you like to come with me?' she asked, trying to make it sound as if she'd only just thought of it. Instead of which, she'd been carrying the leaflet around all day, thinking of little else. 'It would be a great way to practise your English. And it's a really good play.'

'Ah, a play. Shakespeare,' he said. 'Now him I hear about.'

She laughed. 'No, it's not by Shakespeare. A bit more modern than that. It's by a writer called Agatha Christie. I think you'd enjoy it. I love a good murder mystery.'

'Murder mystery?' He looked puzzled. 'What is that, please?'

'It's a story about when someone kills someone else.' She made a chopping motion with her hand across her throat. 'And the detective — the policeman — has to find out who did it. It's what we call a whodunit.'

'Who done it? A bad man, I think,' he said.

'Well, yes, sometimes,' Isobel agreed. 'But sometimes, you know — well, sometimes it is because the murderer — that's the man, or of course the woman, who does the killing — has been pushed beyond endurance. Do you understand?'

'Endurance?' He seized on the unfamiliar word with all the enthusiasm of a beachcomber finding a fossil.

Isobel thought for a moment as an image of Bradley sneering at her, belittling her, divorcing her, came into her head. 'Maybe he, or she, is married to someone who's cruel to them. Someone who treats them so badly that one day something snaps. It happens. I'm not saying it's right, of course,' she added quickly. 'I just meant that sometimes these things aren't always . . . '

She broke off. She didn't know what she meant, to be honest. Maybe that she knew what it was like to be trapped in an unhappy situation with no easy or obvious way out.

He reached across and touched her gently on the hand. 'You look so very sad,' he said softly, his beautiful dark brown eyes clouded with concern. 'Is not so good for you?'

It was the sympathetic tone that did it. That and the tingle that shot up her arm at his touch. She shook her head, annoyed with herself as she felt tears well up in her eyes. Any minute now she was going to come out with the old cliché about her husband not understanding her.

'Your husband? He hurt you?' he asked softly.

She nodded and saw his eyes harden with anger. 'I should never have married him. It was a big mistake.' She picked up her glass, surprised to see her hand was not quite steady.

'Is a bad man who hurt a lady. Especially a beautiful lady like you. Very bad.'

'It was partly my fault. I made him very angry. Bradley has quite a temper on him when he's crossed.'

'Bradley?' He spoke the name uncertainly. 'Is the name of your husband?'

She nodded.

'And what does he do, this . . . Bradley?'

'He's an accountant. He has an office in that little lane just off the high street. He's under a lot of strain at the moment. Very busy, you understand?'

He nodded. 'And is he a big man, this Bradley of yours?'

The question threw her. 'No, not really. Not as big as you, let's put it that way. Why do you ask?'

'Because I help you. Stop him hurting you.'

'Oh no, I didn't mean — ' She started to explain that she hadn't meant that Bradley hurt her physically, even though there had been a moment, back there in the kitchen just before she'd come out when she'd really thought he might. But before she could do so, she saw movement outside the window and looked up to see a couple of men she recognised as being from Bradley's golf club. They'd just got out of their car and were hurrying across to the pub entrance, eager to get in out of the rain. While the meeting with Antonio was innocent enough, she didn't fancy news of it getting back to Bradley. She didn't want to give him any ammunition when it came to their divorce.

'Goodness, is that the time?' she exclaimed. 'Look, I'm sorry, but I really must be getting back. I'd no idea it was so late.'

She stood up, left her drink unfinished on the table and left by the door that opened out in to the pub garden, which was another way out to the car park. Antonio picked up the leaflet from the theatre and hurried out after her.

10

Conor shook the rain off his coat as he walked into the bar of the Nag's Head. It was so crowded that he had some difficulty making his way across. Nevertheless, he saw Lauren straight away. She was sitting on her own, staring down into her glass. She looked far from happy.

'Hi there,' he said. 'We meet again.' *Nice one, Conor,* he thought. Next thing, he'd be asking her if she came here often. What was it about this particular woman that made him act like an awkward teenager when he was anywhere near her? It wasn't like he was attracted to her or anything like that. Besides, getting involved with one of the locals was the last thing he wanted. Getting involved with anyone, come to that.

But before she could answer, the big

bruiser of a guy who'd been playing darts came across. 'You want in, Lolly?' he asked, holding out a set of darts towards her. 'How about I let you win this time?'

She stood up. 'Not tonight, thanks, Scott. This is Conor, by the way. He works in the office. Conor, this is Scott.'

The two men nodded at each other, and even from this distance Conor could feel the unspoken message in Scott's eyes. It couldn't have been plainer if he'd stuck a sign on Lauren's forehead that read 'hands off'.'

'Nice meeting you, Scott,' he said as he moved away. 'See you tomorrow, Lauren.'

Keri, the red-headed barmaid, was watching as he made his way to the bar. The smile she gave him was a whole heap friendlier than the look he'd received from Scott.

'Scott was giving you the hands-off treatment, I see,' she said with a laugh. 'Mind you, you won't want to argue with him. He's as tough as he looks

— and is a holy terror on the rugby pitch. And off it, from what I hear. Your usual?'

'Please.' Conor pulled up a bar stool. 'Are they an item then? Scott and Lauren?'

She gave him a bold, challenging look. 'Why do you ask? You interested?'

'In Scott?' He shook his head. 'I'm not that way inclined.'

Keri gave a shriek of laughter. 'I meant Lauren, of course.'

'The answer's still no. Apart from anything else, I work with Lauren and never mix work and play.' He tried not to think about what had nearly happened between them in the office this morning, how close he'd come to making a complete idiot of himself.

'Now me, I never mind mixing work and play,' Keri murmured with a slow, sultry smile. 'And you know what they say about all work and no play, don't you?'

'Well, this Jack's a pretty dull boy, I can tell you,' Conor said with a smile.

147

'Oh, I wouldn't say that.'

She was a bit on the obvious side, but friendly enough, and always ready to answer his questions. 'Plenty have,' he said with a grin.

'Anyway, you were asking if Scott and Lauren were an item,' she went on as she placed his pint in front of him. 'Lauren always insists they're just good friends; and yet, just now when I was collecting glasses, I couldn't help overhearing them planning to buy a house together. In Jubilee Terrace, of all places.'

Conor froze, the glass half way to his lips. 'Jubilee Terrace?'

'It's a row of poky little houses just off the high street. Not far from where Lauren lives at the moment, actually. I suppose she thinks it'll be handy for keeping an eye on her dad, what with him being on his own and everything.' She looked closely at him and frowned. 'Is something wrong with the beer? It's a fresh barrel, so it should be OK.'

'No, no, the beer's fine,' Conor said,

although he'd suddenly lost his taste for it. Instead, he was remembering what he'd read this morning. Remembering, too, that he'd persuaded himself there was probably an innocent explanation for it.

Only now he wasn't so sure.

★   ★   ★

The next morning, it was a little after 8 o'clock as Lauren hurried up the high street, her head bent against the driving rain. The foul weather matched her mood. She should never have let Scott talk her into staying in the pub last night and having that extra drink, as she now had the headache from hell. It was her own fault. She should have stuck to her decision to go home and have an early night. But seeing Conor cosying up to Keri last night had been unsettling; and when Scott had talked her into a game of darts, she'd given in.

She thought back to that moment of madness with Conor in the office the day before. Even now, the memory of it made her cheeks burn. Thank goodness she'd come to her senses and stepped back at the last minute, before she made a complete idiot of herself.

She checked her watch and pulled her coat collar up higher. She couldn't afford to be late this morning, and had slipped unnoticed past Elsie's house, which was something. As she went past Peas and Cues, she was surprised to see Den wasn't in the shop yet. He always went to the wholesaler's later than everyone else so he could pick up all the less than perfect items that no one else wanted at knock-down prices. But he was usually in the shop before 8, carefully arranging everything so that the bruises and soggy bits didn't show.

She pulled her coat collar closer as she turned into the road where Bradley's office was. It was a narrow lane that this morning acted like a wind tunnel. She shivered and felt really sorry for a runner who was coming the other way. His running kit afforded him little protection against the weather, and his dark hair was plastered to his head as the rain ran down his face. Whatever he was in training for, she thought, must be important to drag him outside on such an awful morning. She gave him a sympathetic smile as they passed each other.

When she reached the office a whole six minutes early, she stared in astonishment as she saw why she hadn't been waylaid by Elsie as she'd passed her house. Elsie was turning away from the office's front door.

Lauren was shocked at the change in her. She always looked good for her age, very upright and sprightly. But now it was as if she'd aged overnight. Not only that, but she looked as if she'd shrunk. And Elsie was usually so careful to keep her neatly permed hair covered in the rain. At the first hint of rain, out would come the folded plastic hat without which she never went any-where. Except, of course, that morning. Her hair was like an unravelling Brillo pad and she didn't even notice.

'Elsie? What's wrong? Are you ill?'

Elsie shook her head.

'Look, come in out of the rain,' Lauren said. 'You're getting soaked. What are you doing here? Did you want to see Bradley? He should be in. At least, he'd better be after all the fuss he made. Come on in, please.'

But Elsie made no move to do so. Instead, she stood on the doorstep while water from a blocked gutter dripped unheeded onto her back.

'Oh Lauren, I'm that upset. I don't know whether I'm coming or going, and that's the truth.' She fished into the suitcase-sized handbag she always toted around with her and took out a crumpled piece of paper. Her hand was shaking as she waved it at Lauren. 'This came in the post this morning. From him.' She jerked her thumb in the direction of Bradley's upstairs office.

'From Bradley? But why? What was it about?'

A shadow passed over Elsie's face. 'It

says — he says — I've got to go.'

'I don't understand. Go where?' Lauren asked. 'And what's it got to do with him?'

'He says I've got to leave my house.' She looked bewildered, and her eyes had none of their usual fire. 'He — he says that some company he acts on behalf of now owns the whole of Jubilee Terrace — I was only renting my cottage, you know — and now it's all going to be demolished so that they can build starting homes, whatever they are.'

'I think you'll find it's starter homes,' Lauren said. 'But that's outrageous. He can't do that. Let me read the letter.'

Lauren and Elsie stepped into the hallway out of the rain as Lauren quickly scanned the letter, the anger rising in her as she did so.

'He can't do that,' she said as she handed Elsie the letter back. 'You're a sitting tenant, and as far as I know there are rules protecting sitting ten-ants. This is probably a mistake. Look, come on, I'll make you a cup of tea and then we'll go up and see Bradley together.'

Elsie shook her head. 'No, I won't, if it's all the same with you. I was going to have it out with him. Got as far as opening the door, but there was no one around, and I couldn't make anyone hear, so I don't think he's there.'

'Really?' Lauren was surprised. 'He insisted that I was here by 8.15 and now he's late. And he had the cheek to go on at me. So what are you going to do? I really think it might pay you to consult a solicitor.'

'I'm going to go back home, then see if I can get hold of my Tom. Talk it through with him.'

'That would be best.' Elsie's son, Tom, lived a three-hour drive away, but he visited as often as he could.

'I'll be off home, Lauren,' Elsie said. 'You know, I never liked that Bradley Northcott. Even when he was a young boy, he was a bit of a handful, with quite a nasty streak. He was and still is a bully, and one of these days someone's going to give him what he deserves.'

Lauren watched her go. She gave a little shiver as she realised that for the first time ever, Elsie looked her age. She'd been part of Lauren's life for so long, she didn't want to think of her getting old.

Lauren took her wet coat off and went upstairs to check if, in fact, Bradley was in after all. The door to his office was closed, which was unusual. Most times, unless he was with a client, it would be propped open with that annoying stone on which Lauren had stubbed her toe on several occasions, so that he could hear what was going on downstairs.

She opened the door, gave a gentle tap, and went in. He was sitting at his desk, but he was obviously no more a morning person than she was, because he'd nodded off, his head resting on his arms. Lauren coughed loudly, but he was so sound asleep he didn't stir. She thought about letting sleeping bosses lie, but she wanted him to know that she was on time for once, so she coughed again and moved closer.

But something wasn't right. Something about the angle of his head made the hair on the back of her neck stand up and her breathing quicken. She took a step closer. And froze.

There was a reason Bradley hadn't looked up as she came in. He couldn't.

He was lying face down in a pool of blood.

11

Lauren didn't scream. She didn't run away. She didn't do any of those things people do on TV. Instead, she stood there, frozen. Unable to move while her brain struggled to make sense of what what her eyes were telling her. But nothing made sense and everything seemed far away, like she was looking down the wrong end of a telescope.

'Are you OK, Bradley?' she croaked; but as soon as she'd said it, she realised it was a particularly dumb thing to say when anyone with half a brain could see he was anything but. Although she wished she hadn't thought about half a brain, because . . .

She took a step closer, then yelled out in pain. It was that wretched stone again. How many more times was she going to kick it? 'Fancy leaving that lying around in the middle of the floor,' she muttered. 'That could be really dangerous.'

But even that didn't snap her out of the weird fugue-like state. She had no idea how long she would have stood there, rubbing her toe and muttering like a madwoman, if she hadn't heard a door open upstairs. She backed out of Bradley's office and went to the bottom of the narrow uncarpeted stairway that led up to the top storey.

'Lauren? I thought I heard voices. You're in early,' Conor called down. 'I'm surprised. You were still knocking them back when I left the pub last night. It must be the overtime you're after. Is Bradley not in yet?'

Lauren tried to tell Conor that Bradley was sort of in but wasn't. That he was in but he was dead. And that she wasn't feeling herself either, although she was obviously a whole lot better than Bradley. But although the words whirled round and round inside her headwith a speed that left her dizzy, they never quite reached her mouth.

Instead, she settled for pointing over her shoulder at Bradley, although she couldn't quite bring herself to turn round and look at him.

'What's wrong? You look like you've seen a ghost. Are you OK? Hang on, I'm coming down.' Conor clattered down the stairs, then stopped abruptly as he saw what she was pointing at. He pushed past her and kicked the stone as well, sending it skittering across the doorway. 'Oh, dear Lord — '

'I — I stubbed my toe on it as well,' Lauren went on, but Conor wasn't listening. Instead, he was staring down at Bradley, his face slack with shock.

'It's the stone Bradley uses as a doorstop. I shouldn't have left it there,' Lauren said, figuring that as long as she kept talking, she wouldn't have to think about the way the pool of blood had spread like a slick of oil across the green leather-topped desk. And how upset Bradley would have been at the sight of it. 'I'll move it right out of the way before someone does themselves a serious injury on the stupid thing.'

As she bent down, she saw the glint of something metallic on the floor. It wasn't a coin but a small copper shield, no bigger than a 10p piece, with a pin fastening on the back. She knew even before she turned it over what she would find on the front. Etched into the copper was the outline of a stag's head. She recognised it because it had belonged to her mother. But what was on earth was it doing here, of all places? She reached out a hand.

'Don't.' Conor's voice shocked her into immediate stillness. 'Don't touch anything. Have you called an ambulance?'

'Ambulance?' Her brain still wasn't functioning. She scrambled to her feet and forced herself to take another look at Bradley. 'You mean he's not dead? But I thought — '

'I'm not a doctor. And he sure as hell looks in a pretty bad way. But he's still breathing.' He bent over to look closer at Bradley. 'Tell them he's unconscious but breathing steadily. That he has a wound to the back of his head and there's some bleeding from his nose.'

'Right,' she muttered as she moved away. 'Head wound. Bleeding from his nose. Unconscious.'

'And Lauren?' he called after her. 'Be sure to ask for police and ambulance, won't you?'

'The p-police?' she stammered. 'But surely — '

'Just do it, Lauren,' he said. 'Use the phone downstairs rather than this one. Best not to touch anything at all in here. Make sure they know it's an emergency. Go on. Hurry.'

Lauren ran down the stairs, made the call then reluctantly went back up to Bradley's office. She didn't want to go back in that room, but she didn't want be on her own either.

'They're on their way,' she told Conor. 'They said not to move him or anything. Just make sure his breathing isn't restricted. Do you think we should be doing mouth to mouth or something? I — I forgot to ask.'

161

'No,' he said. 'There's always a danger of spinal injury with a head wound, which is why they said not to move him. Besides, his breathing, though a bit laboured, is very regular. Let's just hope they're not too long. If he starts coming round before the medics get here, he could do untold damage to himself. We'll have to be ready to restrain him in that case.'

'But they could be ages. The police only come around Stoneford every other Friday night. We don't see them from one week to the next otherwise, except when they're out on the bypass with their speed gun, revenue collecting. Makes you wonder what we pay our taxes for.' She broke off as she saw the expression on Conor's face. 'I'm sorry.' She wiped a shaking hand across her face. 'I'm talking rubbish. It's what I do when I'm stressed. Sorry.'

'Don't be, Conor said. 'But let's hope the ambulance gets here soon.'

Bradley had slumped forward onto his desk, his face turned to one side as if he was sleeping. Lauren hadn't even noticed the trickle of blood from his nose until Conor had mentioned it, but now wondered how she could have missed it. A vivid slash of scarlet against the unnatural pallor of his skin. 'How do you think it happened? He must have slipped and fell. Banged his head on the desk as he did so.'

'Except the wound is at the back of his head,' Conor said. 'From the way he's fallen forward, I'd say he was struck very hard from behind, with the proverbial blunt instrument.'

The initial rush of relief Lauren had felt on learning that Bradley wasn't dead vanished as the implication of Conor's words hit her like a blow to the stomach. The fact that Bradley wasn't dead was no thanks to the person who had very coldly and deliberately hit him on the back on the head. But who? And with what?

She looked down at the grapefruit-sized rock that was still lying in the middle of the floor where Conor had kicked it. It would fit neatly in to a person's hand, and was heavy enough to crush a man's skull if used with sufficient force. For the first time, she saw that there was a smear of what looked like blood on it — and if Conor hadn't stopped her, it would have had her fingerprints all over it. She owed him one. Thank goodness he'd been thinking for both of them.

But before she could say anything, there was a wail of sirens outside. 'Oh thank God, thank God,' she breathed as she hurried downstairs to let the paramedics in.

She was relieved when they came in, took charge and told her and Conor to wait in the office downstairs.

'Do you want a cup of tea or anything?' Conor asked as he followed her into Reception, but she shook her head. She wrapped her arms around her body and perched on the spindly chair near the window, which was as uncomfortable as it looked. The rain was coming down as hard as ever, making it difficult to see out of the window as she kept a lookout for the police.

'Do you think he's going to be all right?' she asked.

Conor shrugged. 'Like I said, head injuries are tricky things. I feel happier now the medics are here. He's in good hands.'

'You seem to know an awful lot about medical stuff,' she said.

'Not really. But my mother's a nurse back in Ireland. And the company I worked for in London was very keen on everyone doing first-aid courses. I've been on several.'

'Thank God you were here,' Lauren said with feeling. 'I don't know what I'd have done if you hadn't been. I'd probably still be standing there now, asking him if he was all right and wondering why he wasn't answering. I — I just froze.'

'Don't beat yourself up about it. It must have been a terrible shock for you, finding him like that,' Conor said. 'How long had you been here before I came in?'

'I — I don't know.' Lauren was still finding it very difficult to focus. 'Not long, I don't think. A couple of minutes, maybe? I'd come in early because Bradley was going to talk me through a job he wanted me to do and — ' She stopped, her cheeks burning as she saw Conor frown. 'He — he didn't want you to know about it. Probably knew how overworked you were and didn't want to add to your burden.'

He gave a short, bitter laugh. 'I doubt that very much. What was it, did he say? It wouldn't be Stag Holdings by any chance?'

Stag? The words sent her thoughts skittering back to her mother's copper brooch that she'd found close to Bradley's desk.

'Stag Holdings?' She shook her head and felt the colour rise in her cheeks. 'He — he didn't say anything about that. Just something about me being

company secretary. But that you — '
Her voice rose with indignation as she
remembered. 'You didn't think I was up
for the job, apparently.'

'I said no such thing. That man really
is a complete — ' he began angrily, then
looked up at the ceiling. 'Jeez, what am
I like? The law will have me down as
suspect number one if I carry on like
that.'

'Of course they wouldn't,' Lauren
said firmly. 'You could never do
something like that.'

'Ah, but how would you be knowing
that?' Conor said softly. 'When you
don't really know me at all.'

'I just know. It must have been a
robbery that went horribly wrong. In
fact, the front door was open when I
arrived.' *And Elsie Thornton was just
coming out! Elsie? Of course not. Not
in a million years*. Lauren pushed the
ridiculous thought aside. The shock had
obviously addled her brain. And where
were the police?

'The front door is always open,'

Conor was saying while these thoughts were racing through Lauren's mind. 'I'm forever telling Bradley it's not a good idea and that he should be more security conscious. But you know what he's like. He won't be told.' He broke off and looked at her closely. 'Are you sure you're all right, Lauren? You're very pale.'

'I don't feel so good. I think I just want to go h-home.' She started to shiver, feeling like she'd just spent the night cuddled up to an iceberg.

'Sure you do. But it's best you wait until the police get here.' He came up to her and put his pinstriped jacket around her shoulders. It felt warm and comforting, and she hugged it to herself like a security blanket. 'They'll be here soon. Are you sure you don't want that cup of tea?'

His smile reminded her, even at such an inappropriate time, why she'd thought he looked like Benedict Cumberbatch the first time they'd met.

Talk about bad timing, she thought

wryly. The story of her life. Especially as the second she smiled back, the wail of sirens yanked her from what could have been one of those beautiful moments you dream about and back into the nightmare of Bradley's poor broken head.

★   ★   ★

The police arrived at the same time as the paramedics were coming down the stairs with Bradley strapped to a stretcher. Lauren and Conor watched as they loaded him into the ambulance. The rain was still lashing down, but even so, a small crowd had gathered outside, attracted by the sirens and flashing lights.

'He — he's going to be all right, isn't he?' she asked one of the paramedics.

'He's in good hands, love,' was all he would say as he hurried out behind his colleagues.

It was just as well Conor was there, because he was able to give the paramedics and later the police all the details they needed, including Bradley's wife's phone number. And it was Conor who told them how they'd found Bradley slumped across his desk and about the out-of-place doorstop.

By contrast, Lauren was a mess as the shock began to hit home. She felt like she was going down with the flu, and every time the police asked anything — including something as simple as her name and address — her mind went blank and her head was filled with cotton wool. And the questions didn't stop at her name and address, but got progressively harder. What time did she come in? Did she see anyone? Did anyone see her? How did she get on with Mr Northcott?

After a while, she began to get the panicky feeling that they had her down as suspect number one, not Conor. Which was quite simply ludicrous. She couldn't even bring herself to squash a spider and would spend hours persuading one to climb onto a piece of paper to move it elsewhere. She didn't believe in violence — unless you counted the urge she got to deck Scott's dad every time he dropped hints about 'the patter of tiny football boots'.

And what could she tell the police anyway, that she hadn't already told them over and over again? She didn't know anything. She didn't hear or see anyone. OK, there was that little encounter with Elsie; but the idea of the seventy-eight-year-old woman creeping up the stairs and bashing Bradley over the head was so ridiculous, they'd probably laugh at her for mentioning it and tell her she'd been watching too many episodes of *Midsomer Murders*.

Eventually, after what seemed like ten hours but was probably only one, they must have realised they weren't going to get any more sense out of her and agreed she could go home, by which time the place was crawling with people in paper suits.

12

Isobel left the house just before 8 o'clock. It was only half an hour's drive to the country club, and she was way too early for her one-to-one training session with Antonio, but she was anxious to get out of the house. And away from Bradley.

But she needn't have bothered, because when she got out to the large triple garage, she realised his car — a dark blue top-of-the-range BMW — was no longer there. He'd obviously already left for the office, although she hadn't heard him go.

She got into her car and, out of habit, checked her appearance in the mirror before starting the engine. She felt pretty grim. In fact, if she was due to see anyone other than Antonio this morning, she'd have cancelled — and even then, she was having doubts. She looked as bad as she felt and was not at all sure she wanted him to see her like this. When she was younger, she could stay up and party all night long and look no worse for it in the morning. But now, it seemed that every restless minute, every moment spent tossing and turning was written in the wrinkles on her face, in the dark shadows under her eyes, in the pallor of her skin.

She couldn't get Bradley's furious expression out of her mind. They hadn't got on for some years now, and she knew she often got on his nerves. But at that moment he'd looked at her as if he hated her. As if he could kill her.

She shivered and turned up the car's heater as far as it would go. How stupid she'd been to antagonise him like that. As for threatening him, what had she been thinking of?

Last night, she'd tried to apologise, tell him she didn't mean it, that she would never threaten him, even if she knew something — which she didn't.

173

That she'd just been winding him up. But he wouldn't listen and in the end she'd given up, gone up to her room and spent the rest of the night trying not to think about what she would do if he carried out his threat.

But, of course, there was no 'if' about it. Sure, he was going to go ahead with his plans to divorce her. Once Bradley decided on a course of action, he had no reverse gear. She'd known that about him for years, and at one time had found it quite an admirable trait. But not anymore.

But by the time the first fingers of dawn lightened the night sky, she'd become resigned to the idea of divorce. Quite resigned, too, to walking away from the expensive house, the luxury car. Well, more than resigned. She was almost looking forward to it in a weird way. Since she'd met Antonio, she was coming to realise that there was truth, after all, in the old cliché that money didn't buy you happiness. Although if it hadn't been for Bradley's money, she'd never have met Antonio in the first place.

Of course, she admitted as she drove off towards Stoneford Manor, she may well be reading too much into their relationship — if, that was, there was a relationship at all. She'd had plenty of time to think that through as well during the long night. But even if things didn't work out as she hoped between them, she was still ready to leave Bradley. If last night had taught her nothing else, it had made her realise that she'd never really known the man she'd been married to for the last sixteen years.

Her low mood lifted slightly by the time she reached the country club. The automatic doors swished open with a discreet hiss as she approached them.

'Good morning, Mrs Bradley.' The sleek blond receptionist on the desk smiled at her, then looked back down at the screen in front of her, a small frown puckering her immaculately drawn brows. 'You're here for your one-to-one with Antonio? I'm sorry, there's been some sort of mix up. We have you in for 9.30. I'm afraid Antonio isn't here yet.'

'No, it's OK. There's no mistake. I'm ridiculously early. I thought I'd go and have a coffee and a skim through the papers first. What a terrible morning.'

The receptionist pulled a face. 'They're forecasting rain for the rest of the day, I'm afraid. I was surprised to see Antonio leave earlier for his morning run. Usually he hates the rain and is always grumbling about it.'

'Isn't he just?' Isobel laughed. 'I'd have thought he'd have used the treadmill on a morning like this. But that's men for you, isn't it? A complete mystery.'

She took her coffee to the table by the window, picked up a newspaper, glanced at the headlines then put it back down again. Nothing but bad news. Like she didn't have enough of her own at the moment.

She glanced out of the window to see Antonio, dressed in running gear, run across the car park towards the accommodation block. His pace was relaxed and he was seemingly unfazed by the driving rain. Her breath caught in her throat at the sight of him. Maybe her life wasn't all bad news after all.

★　★　★

'You were out early this morning,' she said to him later when he joined her in the gym.

'You saw me?' he asked quickly, his brows creased in an anxious frown, his beautiful dark eyes shadowed. 'Where?'

'Why so worried?' she laughed. 'Have you been somewhere you shouldn't have?'

'Of course not,' he said quickly. 'I just wondered where you saw me, that is all.'

'Why, here, of course. I was early and saw you come back from your run. I'm very impressed. You must be dead serious about your training schedule, going out running on such a horrible morning. And here was me thinking you didn't like our English rain.'

He shrugged. 'I don't,' he said, and the expression on his face made it apparent he wasn't in the mood to be teased this morning. 'Now, I thought this morning we increase the weights and introduce a new machine for you to work on. And then we up the speed up the treadmill and go for the cross-trainer. I have special — ' He seemed to be struggling for the word. ' — special thing to show you later. Special routine. We work hard this morning, no?'

She shuddered. She wanted to say no, to explain how a nearly sleepless night had left her feeling every one of her forty-one years. But she wasn't going to tell this twenty-something adonis that. So she took a deep breath and drew on the deepest reserve of her strength.

'Let's do it,' she said. 'On one condition.'

'Oh yes?' He lifted one eyebrow and sent Isobel's pulse through the roof.

'That you agree to come to the theatre with me next week. We talked about it last night, remember?'

He looked across the machine at her, his dark eyes intent, his voice low and urgent. 'I remember we also talked about your husband. How he hurt you. He's a very bad man, no? I help you. I have a plan for — ' He broke off as the door to the gym crashed open and two lycra-clad stick-thin women came in.

'Good morning, Antonio,' they chorused, their faces lit up with flirty smiles that set Isobel's teeth on edge.

'Good morning, ladies.' He smiled back. 'I will be with you in fifteen minutes. Don't forget to warm up properly.'

'I'm warmed up properly just looking at you in that tight T-shirt,' the younger one said, while her friend snorted with laughter.

He shrugged and turned back to Isobel, his manner cool and professional. 'Now this morning, we move on to cross-trainer. Good for leg muscles. I show you.'

★ ★ ★

Conor watched Lauren as she walked down the street. He'd offered to take her home, but she'd refused and assured him that she was perfectly all right, even though he could see she was anything but.

Then he took a deep steadying breath, looked up the number of Isobel Northcott, and keyed it in. It rang for a long time, and he was just beginning to think that voicemail was going to kick in and had decided it was not the sort of thing he could leave as a recorded message, when the call was answered.

'Yes?' She sounded out of breath — and more than a little annoyed.

'Mrs Northcott, this is Conor Maguire here. I'm — '

'What is it, Conor?' she cut in. 'I'm a bit busy at the moment.'

'I realise that. I'm just calling to see if there's anything I can do, and if you'd like a lift to the hospital.'

'The hospital? What are you talking about?'

Conor's heart sank. The police had said they were going to tell her. Obviously they hadn't. 'Look, Mrs Northcott, I'm afraid there's been . . . there's been some sort of accident, and Bradley's been taken to hospital. He's pretty badly hurt, I'm afraid.'

The silence went on for so long that Conor began to think she hadn't heard him. He was just about to repeat what he'd said when she spoke. 'Do you mean a car accident?' Her voice was little more than a whisper. 'Where? What happened?'

'No, not a car accident.' Conor swallowed hard. 'Look, we don't know for sure yet, but the police think he may have been attacked. In fact, they're pretty sure he was. I thought they were going to tell you. I'm sorry; I wouldn't have — '

She gave a sharp intake of breath. 'Attacked? Where?'

'Over the head. It looks like he was

hit from behind.'

'I didn't mean that.' Her voice was shrill and panicky. 'I meant, where did the attack — if that's what it was — happen?'

'Oh, sorry. It was in the office. This morning. Lauren came in at just after 8 and found him.'

'Just after 8?' Her voice rose. 'They think he was attacked just after 8?'

'As far as I know, they don't know when the actual attack took place. Only that it was a little after 8 when Lauren found him.'

Her voice sharpened. 'And who's Lauren?'

'She's the young woman who started working here a couple of weeks ago.'

'A young woman?' she snapped. 'How young?'

Shock did strange things to people, Conor thought. What did it matter what age Lauren was? And why hadn't Isobel Northcott even asked which hospital Bradley had been taken to? She was obviously having trouble taking it in.

'The paramedics said they were taking him to Dintscombe Royal Infirmary,' he said gently. 'Would you like me to drive you there? I can be with you in ten minutes.'

'No, I can manage,' she said quickly. Her voice softened. 'I'm — I'm sorry, Conor. I meant to say no thank you. And thank you, too, for telling me. It's ... well, this has come as a shock, that's all. I can't quite ... '

'And I'm sorry to be the bearer of bad news,' he said when he realised she wasn't going to finish the sentence. 'As I said, I'll be happy to — '

'There's no need,' she said briskly. 'I can manage. Thank you.'

With that, the phone went dead, and Conor's screen read 'call ended'.

★ ★ ★

Isobel turned her phone off, dropped it into her handbag and put it back in the locker. Moving as if in a dream, she went through the motions of getting

183

ready for a shower, but her hands were shaking so much she could hardly drag her sports top off. She was thankful she was the only person in the ladies' changing rooms. She needed time to compose herself before she faced anyone. Needed time, too, to sort out what she was going to do.

She couldn't take it in. Bradley. Attacked. In his office. By whom?

'Is bad man. I help you.' Antonio's stumbling words played over and over in her head. Along with the picture of Antonio running in the rain this morning. Antonio, who hated the rain.

She peeled off the rest of her sports clothes, stepped into the shower, and let the needle-sharp water pound her aching body. *Think, think, think, Isobel*, she urged herself. But her brain had turned to cotton wool.

Her legs, too. But whether that was from the shock of Conor's phone call or the punishing routine Antonio had just put her through in the gym, she didn't know. All she *did* know was that for once she was thankful when he'd said it was time to finish. She had made up her mind to tell him that she couldn't do this anymore, that he was pushing her too hard.

'Antonio, I — ' she began, but he cut across her.

'I see you later, yes?' He spoke urgently, his voice low, as he kept one eye on the two giggling women who were waiting for him over by the rowing machines. 'I finish at 2. Maybe we meet?'

Her heart leapt. This was the first time he'd suggested a meeting. 'Of course. When? Where?'

'Later. But not here. In park in Stoneford. You know it?'

Isobel nodded, her heart thudding so loud he must have heard it. 'Of course. But what — ?'

'I tell you later. I have something to show you. Is important. Oh, and wear something . . . *confortavel*.'

'Comfortable,' she prompted, scarcely daring to breathe.

'*Sim*, comfortable.' He enunciated

each syllable carefully.

She'd come into the changing room, dancing on air, all the aches and pains from her session in the gym forgotten. And then she'd heard her phone ringing. Oh, how she wished she'd never answered it.

Of course there was no way she could meet Antonio now. She'd text him later to say so. They had to stay apart, for his sake. Or would a text from her to him incriminate him? What to do?

She was still undecided as she finished her shower, dressed and drove back to the house. As she pulled in to the long gravelled driveway, she saw to her dismay that a police car was already there. A policeman was standing on the doorstep. She got out and walked towards him. He looked very solemn. Was he going to tell her Bradley was dead? Certainly Conor had said it was very serious.

She took a few moments to compose herself. She needed to get this right. Play the distraught, loving wife — or widow — for all she was worth.

And, of course, be ready to give Antonio a false alibi if he needed one.

13

News travelled around Stoneford faster than the norovirus, and Lauren hadn't been home ten minutes when her father phoned.

'I've just heard about Bradley. Are you all right, love?' he asked anxiously. 'Do you want me to come home?'

'No, Dad. I'm fine, honestly,' she said.

Thankfully, he didn't believe her, which was why half an hour later he was fussing and clucking around her like a hen with one chick while she huddled, shivering, in the armchair, really glad of his company.

'Why don't I make you a cup of tea?' he asked for what felt to Lauren like the hundredth time. 'It'll make you feel better, sweetheart.'

But it wouldn't, of course. How could it? Because every time she closed her eyes, she could see Bradley's face as they wheeled him away, his skin the colour of cold porridge, his eyes closed.

She shuddered. 'I'd love a cup of tea, Dad,' she said. She didn't, but figured it would give him something to do and maybe stop him asking her if she was all right every ten seconds or so.

She put her hand in her pocket for a tissue and felt what she thought at first was a coin. But it wasn't. It was the little copper shield with a stag's head on it. How had it come to be in her pocket? The last time she remembered seeing it, it had been on the floor by Bradley's desk.

What had she done? She remembered bending down to move the doorstop when Conor had stopped her, just in time, from what the police would have no doubt seen as contaminating a crime scene. But she'd done far worse than that. She'd removed something from a crime scene, even though for the life of her she had no recollection of having done so. Any more than she could work out what Bradley had been doing with her mother's brooch in the first place.

'I think I'll go upstairs and lie down for a bit, Dad,' she said as he came back in with the tea. 'I'll take it up with me, thanks.'

'Good idea, Kitten.' He was still looking worried. 'Are you sure you don't want me to call Dr Clarke? You've had a nasty shock. He could give you something.'

'I'm sure, Dad. I'll be OK once I've had a sleep.'

He looked so worried that Lauren forced a smile to reassure him, and then went upstairs. But instead of going to bed, she went to her wardrobe and took out a small box with a delicate wooden inlay pattern on the lid. It was her mother's jewellery box, and Lauren hadn't opened it since the day she'd died.

As soon as she lifted the lid of the box, she realised why she'd put it off for so long. She could smell her mother's perfume and hear her soft laugh as she demanded to know what Lauren thought she was doing rootling around her things. And what things. There were her rings, of course, and some long crystal earrings that used to fascinate her when she was little. She'd loved the way they made little dancing rainbows whenever the light caught them as her mother moved her head. There, too, were the hideous red plastic earrings that Lauren had bought her mother with her pocket money when she was about eight. They were wrapped as carefully as if they were rubies set in gold.

Lauren wanted to snap the box shut and push it to the back of the wardrobe until she felt better able to cope with it. She'd had enough trauma for one day. But she also wanted to put the copper brooch back where it belonged.

'I made this years ago,' Lauren remembered her mother once telling her when she'd asked her about it. 'I've made better things, but it's still very precious to me because it represents something I really believed in. Something I was proud of.'

Lou Chapman had been very creative, the ideal person to run a craft shop, which she did in the shop unit next door to Peas and Cues until her illness forced her to give it up. She made lots of beautiful things. Their house was still full of them, but the little stag brooch had always been one of Lauren's favourites.

Of course, she shouldn't have picked it up. She knew that. But she'd done it without really registering what she was doing She knew, too, that she should have handed it over to the police the second she realised what she'd done. But she couldn't bear to see it tossed carelessly on the floor of Bradley's office as if it was just a piece of worthless rubbish. Surely it couldn't have anything to do with the attack on Bradley, she told herself. All she'd wanted to do was put it back where it belonged.

The jewellery box was in two parts. She lifted off the tray that held the smaller items like rings and earrings — and for the second time that day froze.

There in the bottom, nestling among the brooches and beads, was a little copper shield with a stag's head engraved on it. It was identical to the one she held in her hand.

In a day full of bad moments, she realised how very deep in trouble she was, and how she would probably spend the rest of her life sewing mailbags, or whatever they did in women's prisons these days.

She curled up on her bed and cried like she was never going to stop. And when her father came up, saw the state she was in and suggested calling Dr Clarke, this time she didn't argue.

★　★　★

In spite of Dr Clarke's sleeping pills, Lauren spent a restless night and woke next morning still frantic about the copper brooch. She'd managed to convince her dad she was feeling a bit better and that he could do nothing for her by staying at home, because all she was planning to do that day was sleep. Reluctantly, and only after making her promise to ring him if she felt any worse, he'd gone off to work.

She'd just made herself a cup of coffee, and was sitting down to have a good hard think about how she was going to get the brooch back to Bradley's office, when there was a knock on the door. She leapt like a startled rabbit, spilling her coffee all over the table. Was this it? Was it the police already, come to search the house for the missing piece of evidence?

She was so relieved when she eventually plucked up the courage to open the door and found Den standing there that she almost threw her arms around him and kissed his bald spot.

'How are you this morning?' he asked, his little round face creased with anxiety. 'I came as soon as I heard. What a dreadful, dreadful experience for you. If I'd known what was going to happen, I would never have let you go and work for him.'

'And if I'd known, I wouldn't have wanted to go and work for him,' she said fiercely as she mopped up the spilt coffee. 'Do you want some coffee?'

'No, thanks. And if I did, I'd prefer it out of a cup,' he added.

But Lauren wasn't in the mood for Den's jokes that morning. If indeed she ever was. She ignored it and merely rolled her eyes at him as she took a sip of her coffee.

'But is it true what people are saying?' His little piggy eyes gleamed as he asked the question. 'That his skull was smashed open like a watermelon?'

'Den, honestly!' Suddenly the coffee tasted sour in her mouth and she put her cup back down on the table with a bang. 'And shouldn't you be opening up the shop?' She looked pointedly at her watch.

'I'm that worried about Bradley, I can't even think of opening yet,' he said. 'I've tried getting some sense out of the hospital, but they just say he's comfortable, whatever that means. Here, I've brought you some grapes.'

'Thanks.' As she took them, Lauren couldn't help wondering how long they'd been hanging around in the shop. But it was a kind thought.

'I still can't believe it,' Den went on, his mayor-in-waiting way of talking forgotten as he eased himself into the sofa like he was settling down for a good long gossip. 'Did you see anyone? Hear anyone? I suppose the police have already asked you all this?'

'Only a hundred and five times,' Lauren said. 'And my answer was always the same, which must have disappointed them. I'd gone in earlier than usual because Bradley had asked me to, but I didn't see or hear anyone — apart from Elsie Thornton, of course. And I can't see her making it up the stairs to Bradley's office, not with the state of her bunions, can you? Least of all whack him over the head like that. So I didn't bother to tell the police about that.'

Den sat up sharply. 'Elsie Thornton was there? Then no, probably best not to say anything. Although from what I heard, she was pretty upset with Bradley over that notice to quit. Goodness knows why, though. She'd be much better off in a home at her age. I told her it was all for the best.'

'You told her that?' Lauren bristled with indignation on Elsie's behalf. 'For pity's sake, Den, when the good fairy was handing out tact and diplomacy at your christening, I reckoned you'd already done a deal with the bad fairy and traded them in for cash.'

'I just say it like it is,' he said in a tone of injured innocence. 'She's going gaga, you know. You should have heard her the other day when I suggested she might like to try aubergines for a change. You'd think I'd been trying to sell her rat poison, the way she went on.

Old people can be very unpredictable, you know. It's those senior dimensions, I reckon.'

'Not Elsie,' she said firmly. 'Not in a million years. In fact I can't think there's anyone in this town capable of doing such a dreadful thing. The police are treating it as attempted murder, you know.'

'Surely not.' Den's little legs flailed about like streamers in the wind as he struggled to get off the sofa. His round face was quite red with the effort by the time he finally managed to extricate himself. 'Now, if you'll excuse me, Lauren,' he said, tugging his waistcoat back into place over his paunch, 'I'd better go and open up. I can't do anything for Bradley by sitting around here fretting and gossiping, can I? And you never know, there may well be a few gentlemen of the press in town, looking for statements.' He was back in mayor-in-waiting mode again. 'It's my civic duty to be on hand if needed.'

But although Lauren had told Den

she didn't believe the attacker could be anyone from Stoneford, she recalled reading some chilling statistics about how many people were capable of murder, or in this case, attempted murder, given the right set of circumstances. Everyone except Elsie Thornton, of course. Lauren hadn't said anything to the police about seeing her yesterday morning because she knew she couldn't possibly have done it.

She also hadn't told them about the row she'd overheard between Bradley and Conor the other day, and how Conor had countered Bradley's threat of the sack with a threat of his own. She remembered the expression on Conor's face as he'd come out of Bradley's office that day; how angry he'd been. So who was he? And what was a London trained accountant doing working for a small-time one-man business in the back of beyond? Particularly one who didn't seem to appreciate him. It simply didn't make sense.

And that, she realised, was the really

awful thing about an unwitnessed violent assault like the one on Bradley. Until the police caught who did it, she knew she'd find herself suspecting everyone, from the school crossing patrol lady to the vicar.

Of course Conor didn't do it, she told herself fiercely as she shrugged on her jacket. Any more than Elsie had, or the vicar.

She put her hand in her pocket and once again felt the sharp corners of the little copper shield. And, once again, the nightmare of yesterday washed over her.

'Oh, God,' she whispered as panic gnawed at her insides. 'What am I going to do with this?'

14

Conor sat at Lauren's desk in Reception, his hand hovering over the phone. Should he ring her to see how she was this morning? She'd looked terrible when he'd sent her home yesterday, and he still regretted not having insisted on going with her, but the police were still wanting a statement from him and so he'd had to stay. But her pale face and haunted expression had disturbed his sleep last night as much as the memory of finding Bradley.

He'd phoned the hospital earlier that morning, but once they'd discovered he wasn't a member of Bradley's family, they had refused to tell him anything. Only that he was 'comfortable', whatever that meant.

Maybe he'd call Lauren later. He reached across the desk and picked up the scarf she'd left there yesterday. Its

201

silky smoothness slipped through his fingers, a mixture of jewel-bright pinks and purples. He opened the desk drawer and was about to put the scarf in when he noticed her handbag. She'd been in such a state when she'd left, she'd forgotten it. Now he really had a reason to go and see her, which would be better than phoning.

But first things first. He looked down at Bradley's diary, which lay open in front of him. He'd dealt with the two afternoon appointments, both clients that he was familiar with, so he was able to reschedule them for next week. All that was left was a 9.30 appointment for this morning. No name. Just the initials M.S., who was obviously a nonshow as it was now just after 10.

At that moment, the office phone rang. Before he could say anything, an angry voice on the other end said: 'Where the devil are you, Northcott? We agreed 9.30 at the site, didn't we? This was all your damned idea, if you remember. Well, time's money, man, and I've got better things to do than hang around waiting for you to deign to put in an appearance.'

Conor cleared his throat. 'Look, I'm very sorry, Mr — ?' He put in a pause, hoping that the man would supply his name.

But he didn't. Instead, still clearly annoyed, he demanded: 'Who the devil are you?' There was a faint north-country twang to his voice.

'My name's Conor Maguire. And I'm Bradley's . . . his partner. Look, I'm terribly sorry, but I'm afraid Bradley's been in an accident and is in hospital.'

'An accident? Always said the damn fool couldn't handle that fancy car of his.'

Conor didn't bother to put him right. He wound Lauren's silky scarf in and out of his fingers while he chose his words with care. With a bit of luck, he could find something out. 'Is there anything I can do? I'm familiar with all Bradley's cases. We tend to work on things together.'

'Well, there's no point having a site meeting now. Bradley was the one who wanted it, and to be honest I'm more than happy to cut it short today. I've got to be in Bristol before lunch. I just wanted to check with him that the last of the tenants have in fact agreed to move out, and that the application will be passed by planning as promised.'

A bubble of excitement rose in Conor's chest. He gripped the scarf even tighter. 'Everything's going smoothly this end,' he said. 'You needn't worry.'

'Well, I've got my team on standby, just waiting for the nod. I've had a quick look round this morning and there doesn't seem to be any problem with the site. So as soon as we get the go-ahead, we'll be there.'

'Would that be Jubilee Terrace?' Conor said, and instantly knew he'd said the wrong thing.

'I thought you said you were up to speed with this?' the man said sharply. 'Partner or not, I didn't think Bradley would have discussed this project with

204

anyone. I think we're at cross purposes here. So just forget what I said. I'll wait until I can speak to Bradley.'

With that, the line went dead, leaving Conor staring at the phone, his heart thudding. What site were they talking about, then? Obviously not Jubilee Terrace, so that was one theory knocked out of the window. What other pie had Bradley Northcott got his dirty little fingers in? Was it anything to do with Stag Holdings?

He tapped out Isobel's number. 'Good morning, Mrs Northcott,' he said when eventually she answered. 'It's Conor here. From the office. I was just wondering if you had any news of Mr Northcott this morning.'

'No change from yesterday. He's still in a coma and they're still not telling me anything.' The edge of annoyance in her voice vanished as she went on softly, 'But thank you for taking the trouble to phone, Conor. I appreciate it.'

'Is there anything I can do?' he went

on. 'I've got all his meetings covered for the rest of the week. I just wondered if you need a lift to the hospital or anything.'

'I'm quite capable of driving myself, thank you,' she replied sharply, but obviously instantly regretted it because she quickly went on: 'Oh no, no. I'm sorry. I didn't mean that how it came out. Please forgive me for being so rude when you were just being kind.'

'Don't worry. You weren't being rude. You're under a lot of stress and are probably inundated with offers of help. I can assure you, I didn't take offence.'

'And I'm sorry about yesterday too.' She sounded a bit calmer now. 'I was rude then, as well, and yet I was so grateful to you for telling me about the — about the accident. So much better than hearing it from those grim-faced policemen who actually had the nerve to ask me where I was at 8 o'clock yesterday morning. Like they thought I'd done it. But I'm sorry if I came across as ungrateful and rude. Bradley was . . . ' She paused, then went on, 'Bradley's always telling me off for not engaging my brain before opening my mouth. At least, that's the way he puts it.'

'Please don't give it another thought. As for the police asking you where you were yesterday morning, they asked me the very same thing.'

'And where were you?' she asked, her voice sharp again.

'I was in the office. In the room above Bradley's.'

'So who do you think could have done it? Did you see anyone? Hear anything? What did you tell the police?' Her voice rose. 'They must have asked you. After all, you were right there on the spot so to speak. You must have — '

'I told them I didn't hear a thing. Except I heard voices, very quiet. Certainly not raised. And certainly no one I recognised. As to who attacked him, I can assure you, Mrs Northcott, it wasn't me.'

'What? Oh no. I didn't think — I didn't mean to imply — ' Her words came tumbling out. 'You see, there I go again. What am I like? Although, now I think of it, you and Bradley didn't get on very well, did you? And I wouldn't blame you if you had . . . well, you know. Had a go at him, with the way he led you on.'

'I can assure you, I didn't — ' he tried to cut in, but she talked across him.

'He could be a very difficult man to work for. I should know. I worked for him before I married him, so I've seen both sides of him.' There was a small silence. 'Not that I meant to imply that you did it, of course. Only that Bradley has a way of upsetting almost everyone he met.'

'And what did you mean just now?' Conor asked quietly. 'About him leading me on?'

'Well, letting you think you were in line for a partnership when all the time the job was only a temporary one. He was planning to let you go once the end of the tax-year rush was over, you know.'

Conor bit back an exclamation of annoyance. Why should he worry? He never had any intention of staying in the job any longer than he had to. Even so . . .

'Then there was that new woman,' Isobel was saying. 'Lucy, or whatever her name was. Did she hear or see anything?'

'Do you mean Lauren?'

'Something like that. He's going to ditch her, too, as soon as she's served her purpose, you mark my words.'

'So tell me, Mrs Northcott — ' he began, but she cut in again.

'Oh please, Conor. Call me Isobel.'

'Very well. Then tell me, Isobel, does the name Stag Holdings Limited mean anything to you?'

But the line had gone dead, leaving Conor staring down at Lauren's lovely scarf, now scrunched into a tiny ball in his hand.

The chair rasped against the floor as he stood up. He took Lauren's handbag out of the drawer and folded the scarf carefully, trying to smooth out some of the creases. He needed a breath of fresh air — and going to see Lauren would be just that.

He was about to leave the office when the phone rang. It was Lauren.

★   ★   ★

Lauren stared down at the little stag brooch in her hand and fought against the panic that threatened to overwhelm her. The effects of Dr Clarke's sleeping pill had left her with a head full of cotton wool.

Think, Lauren, think, she urged herself as she tried to clear the fog in her mind. But all she could think was that she'd taken the little brooch from a crime scene. She had to get back to the office and put it back. Not where she'd found it, obviously. But maybe she could drop it down the back of a chair or in the kitchen.

She picked up her coat and looked around for her handbag. Where was it? Usually she hung it on the peg next to her coat. So where was it?

Then she remembered. In all the upset of the day before, she'd left it in the office, in her desk drawer, to be precise. It was the excuse she needed. She dialled the office number, and after a few rings Conor answered.

'Lauren, hi. How are you feeling today?' His voice was as soft and soothing as warmed honey.

'Oh well, you know. Still a bit shaky,' she said with a not-very-convincing laugh. 'No, that's not true, actually. I'm still a lot shaky. Dr Clarke gave me something to help me sleep last night and it's left me . . . well, you know. I can't seem to get my head in gear this morning. And — oh, my God. What must you think of me? I haven't asked if there is any news of Bradley this morning.'

'No change this morning. He's still in

a coma. And what I think of you is that you're someone who's dealing with one hell of a shock, and you're doing fine. So don't you go worrying about it.'

'That's very kind of you to say so. And I'm so glad you're in the office. I wasn't sure if anyone would be. You see, I can do with a walk and a bit of fresh air to clear my head. And I've just realised I left my handbag in my desk drawer yesterday. It's got my phone in it and everything, so I thought I'd pop round to pick it up. I was just checking to make sure someone will be in the office when I get there, that's all.'

'Sure. But look, I've got about another hour here and then I'm done. I'm just ringing around those clients who have got assessments coming up, or appointments with Bradley, and keeping them in the picture. Save you coming in, I could bring it round to you if you can do without it for another hour. Would you prefer that?'

Too right she'd prefer that, she thought grimly. If she had the choice, she'd never set foot inside that dreary office ever again. But she had to return that shield, even though the thought of going back to the office made her feel sick. As for walking in and seeing those stairs leading up to Bradley's office . . .

'No, you've got enough to do,' she forced herself to say. 'I'll be fine, honest. And like I said, I could do with some fresh air. The walk will do me good.'

The second she put the phone down, it rang. She thought for a moment it might be Conor calling her back. But it was Scott.

'Why aren't you answering your mobile?' he grumbled.

'Oh, hi Lauren. How are you feeling this morning?' she said, laying on the sarcasm.

'Yeah, well, sorry,' he mumbled. 'So how are you?'

'Fine,' she said sharply. 'Look, Scott, I'm in a hurry. I've got to go in to the office and — '

'Are you mad?' His bellow was so

loud that Lauren moved the phone away from her ear. 'You're not going anywhere near that place again, Lolly. I forbid you.'

There were so many things wrong with that response on so many levels. The least of them being that the volume had set her ears ringing.

'You what?' Lauren's voice, like her hackles, rose sharply. 'Did you just say what I thought you said?'

'Well, I told you that working there was a rubbish idea, didn't I?' he muttered.

'Oh, right. You knew I was going to find Bradley with his head bashed in, did you?' she said, even though she knew that sarcasm was wasted on Scott.

'Of course not. How could I? Oh and by the way, Mum said to tell you she'll be around later with some of her special rhubarb rum. She says it's just the thing for shock.'

'A shock to my entire nervous system, more like,' Lauren said with feeling, having suffered the after-effects of Sandra Wilde's homemade wines on several never-to-be-forgotten occasions.

'So come on, Lolly, give,' he said. 'Mum says to ask you if — '

'This isn't about you ringing up to see how I am at all, Scott Wilde, is it?' she snapped. 'You called because your mum wants a bit of gossip ahead of the pack. Well, I'm very sorry to disappoint the pair of you, but I didn't see anything. And if I did, I wouldn't tell you. Or your mum. Now, I've got to go.'

As soon as she put the phone down, she regretted speaking so sharply to him. He meant well, even if his mum didn't. She rummaged around in the drawer for the spare house key (hers was still in her handbag, she hoped, but just in case) and promised herself that she'd call Scott when she got back and maybe suggest meeting up for a drink this evening.

As she approached Jubilee Terrace, she noticed that the For Sale sign had disappeared from the house next to Elsie's and hoped that Scott hadn't bought it. But then she remembered how Elsie had told her that Bradley's company now owned the whole terrace. What would happen to it if Bradley died? But, of course, he wasn't going to die, she told herself sharply. Den had said he was 'comfortable', didn't he? They wouldn't have told him that if he was about to die, would they?

As she passed Elsie's house, she was surprised to see her front door open, which was weird. Dooley was in his customary lookout point in the front room window, but his barking was even more manic than usual.

She pushed open the front door cautiously, knowing from past experience how unreliable Dooley's temper could be when he was roused. And he certainly sounded more roused than she'd ever heard him.

'Good dog, Dooley. Hi, Elsie — it's only me . . . ' she called, but stopped, a horrible feeling of déjà vu rushing over her.

Elsie was lying face down on the

floor, her steel-grey curls a stark contrast to the scarlet stain that was pooled around her head. Bending over her was Conor, who whirled round at the sound of Lauren's horrified cry.

His hands, not to mention the cuffs of his usually immaculate white shirt, were covered in blood.

15

Isobel dropped the phone on the kitchen table and looked across at the remains of last night's bottle of wine. Was it too soon? Certainly it had helped to soothe her jangled nerves last night when she'd come back from the hospital, the memory of that last encounter with that po-faced policeman, the one who'd wanted to know where she was at 8 o'clock yesterday morning, still raw.

Yes, of course it was too soon for a drink. She had to drive to the hospital again today. And there was always the chance she might be able to see Antonio later. She needed to see him, to look in to his eyes while she told him what had happened to Bradley.

Did she really think Antonio had done it? And, if he had, how did she feel about it? Hadn't he promised to help her with what he called 'that bad man'? Had he taken matters into his own hands? And if so, how did she feel about that?

She sat down at the table and picked up her phone again. No missed calls. No messages. She tapped in his number and drummed her fingers on the table as she waited for him to answer. She was about to end the call when he did so.

'Antonio. It's Isobel here.'

'Isobel?' He sounded distracted and out of breath — and was that a woman's soft laugh she could hear in the background? A flash of jealousy stabbed Isobel like a knife. Who was he with? And what were they doing?

'Isobel Northcott,' she said curtly. 'You asked to meet me yesterday afternoon and I texted you to say I couldn't make it, remember?'

'Ah, *sim, sim*. Yes, for sure I remember. Of course. I'm sorry. I am come ... no, not right. My bad English. I have come from my running.

Early morning. So sorry.'

'No, no, nothing to be sorry for. I just wanted to let you know that I couldn't see you yesterday afternoon because I was at the hospital. And then I had to deal with the police. It was quite a day, I can assure you.'

'Hospital? Police? You are hurt? In accident?'

Isobel was gratified by the level of concern in his voice, and her flash of irritation melted away. 'No, I'm fine, thank you. I . . . ' She thought about telling him about the attack on Bradley but decided against it. She needed to see his face when she told him. Then she would know. 'I — I was wondering if I could meet you today instead?' she asked.

'Today? Not possible. I'm sorry. I have — I work all morning.'

'And this afternoon? After you finish work?'

'I have — I have to go. Go see . . . ' She heard the frustration in his voice as he struggled to find the right words, muttering something in Portuguese she didn't understand.

'Never mind,' she said. 'I'll see you tomorrow in the gym, as we agreed. OK?'

'OK. I look forward to it, Isobella.'

There. He was doing it again. That little pause in the middle of her name. Is-so-bella. He made it sound like a poem, and a million miles away from the ugly 'Izzy' that Bradley insisted on calling her, even though — or, more likely, because — he knew she hated it.

'Antonio,' she said quickly before he could ring off, 'have — have you seen the police?'

'I'm sorry?' He sounded panicky. 'The police? Why? All my papers are good. I'm not illegal, you know. All good, my papers.'

'Oh no, of course you're not illegal. I didn't for a moment think otherwise. It's just that maybe sometime the police will ask you things. Where you were at a certain time, things like that. And — and it's not always easy to remember, is it? Like when you go out running, for instance. It's easy to forget where you went or who you saw.'

'Ah no. Is easy for me. I keep a running . . . how you call it? A running book. Record all my runs for my training. I never forget. Write them all in book.'

'And yesterday?' she asked. 'Do you remember where you went yesterday morning? Or maybe you didn't run at all. It was raining, wasn't it? And you hate the rain, don't you?'

'I ran. In the rain. Is in my book.'

'And did you see anyone when you were out in the rain, or did anyone see you?'

'Why do you ask?' There was a sharp, panicky edge to his voice that made Isobel uneasy. 'Is this what police ask? Why? I don't understand.'

She gave up. 'I'll maybe explain when I see you. Just forget about it, OK? Nothing to worry about.'

Nothing for him to worry about, maybe, but plenty for her. What if

Bradley died? Wasn't there a thing called incitement to murder? Was that what she'd done?

'But I didn't mean to,' she said out loud to the empty room as the panic rose in her throat. 'I didn't mean for Antonio or anyone, come to that, to attack him. Oh God, this is all my fault. What am I going to do?'

She made herself a double-strength cup of coffee and forced herself to calm down. Of course Antonio didn't do it. Why would he? It was probably just a passing tramp. Maybe he'd bedded down for the night in the office and Bradley had disturbed him.

'Don't let Bradley die,' she whispered. 'Please don't let him die. I know I said I wanted to be free of him, and I do. I really do. I don't love him anymore, if indeed I ever did. And he certainly doesn't love me. Never has done. But I don't want it to end like this. I don't even care about the money anymore.'

As she inhaled the fragrant steam of

the strong hot coffee, her head began to clear. No, she didn't want Bradley to die, and yes, she did want out of this loveless marriage. And to her surprise, she realised that in fact she really, really didn't care about the money anymore. It hadn't brought her happiness. In fact, if she was honest, she'd been bored out of her mind these last few years.

Bradley said she couldn't earn enough to support herself, but he was wrong, of course. Like he was about most things about her. She could get a job, maybe even in the country club. That way she could still see Antonio. Always providing, of course, he wasn't in prison for assault — or worse.

She finished her coffee and began to get her things together ready for the trip to the hospital. As she was about to leave, the phone rang.

'Mrs Northcott,' the soft voice on the other end of the line said. 'It's Sister Marchant from the hospital here . . . '

16

'Lauren, don't just stand there.' Conor's urgent voice barely penetrated the roaring in her ears. 'I said call an ambulance.'

'I — I — can't — n-no ph-phone.' Her attempt to explain that she didn't have her phone with her simply came out as a garbled mess.

But Conor must have somehow understood her, because he tossed his phone at her, then turned back to Elsie who, to Lauren's immense relief, was beginning to stir. Her long low moan brought Dooley racing towards her, barking furiously.

'It's all right, Elsie,' Conor said in quiet soothing voice. 'You've had a bit of a tumble by the look of you. Best not to move for a bit, OK?'

For the second time in as many days, Lauren called 999. As soon as the call was made and she had been assured that the ambulance was on its way, she knelt down beside Elsie and took her hand. Dooley started barking again, this time even louder than before. In the confined space of Elsie's small hall, it made Lauren's ears ring. But at least it seemed to be getting through to Elsie, who stirred restlessly.

'What's the dog's name?' Conor asked. 'Let's get him to shut up, shall we?'

'It's Dooley. But once he starts barking, he doesn't stop. He — '

'Dooley. Quiet.' Conor said in a calm but firm voice. 'Sit down. There.'

And to Lauren's amazement, the dog did exactly that. He sat in the corner Conor had pointed at and looked up at him, his bright little eyes shining with adoration.

'How did you do that?' she asked. 'Dooley doesn't shut up for anyone. As for sitting, I didn't know he knew what the word meant.'

'Growing up like I did with a ton of

older sisters, I learnt from an early age how to make myself heard,' he said with a sudden smile that made her pulse quicken. Then he leaned towards Elsie. 'It looks like she might be coming round.'

'It's Lauren here, Elsie. You're going to be fine. Just fine.' Lauren was pleasantly surprised at how confident she sounded, certainly a lot more confident than she felt. 'Don't worry. The ambulance is on its way.'

'Oh no, no, no . . . No ambulance. No hospital,' Elsie whimpered as she struggled to sit up. 'I can't — '

Conor put a gently restraining hand on her shoulder. 'Please don't try and move, at least not until the paramedics have seen you. Just in case. Do you have a blanket or anything we can put around you to make you more comfortable?'

'There's one in the sitting room,' Lauren said and hurried to fetch it, relieved to be doing something.

'We'll just put this here, then.' With

great gentleness, Conor put the blanket over Elsie. 'There now, that's better. You're going to be fine, so you are. I promise.'

'I . . . remembered you,' she said faintly as she looked up at him. Her eyes, usually bird-bright were now soft and unfocussed.

'Sure you did,' he said. 'But for now, you just lie still. And don't try to talk.'

'The funeral . . . ' she said as her blue-veined eyelids fluttered and closed. Her face sagged and Lauren's heart skipped a beat. Had she passed out again? And why was she talking about funeral arrangements? Surely she wasn't . . . She didn't think she was going to . . .

'Would — would you like me to contact Tom?' Lauren said quickly, and breathed a sigh of relief when Elsie's eyes snapped open. They were a little clearer but still a long way from the vivid blue they normally were.

'No need to call him.' Her voice was stronger now, with only a hint of the earlier tremor. 'He's already on his way.

I phoned him yesterday and he said he'd come down today. Oh dear, Lauren, what will he think when he gets here and finds I'm not here? He'll be that worried.'

'Now don't you go fretting about that. I've got his mobile number. I'll call him and explain. And don't worry about Dooley either,' Lauren went on, looking down at the little dog who was fidgeting anxiously. He was still in the spot Conor had directed him to — but only just. And his frantic barking had muted to an anxious whine. 'I'll take him home with me. You'll like that, won't you, Dooley? Funny thing, I was going to drop by later today to see if he fancied a walk.'

'You're a good woman, Lauren,' Elsie whispered, her eyelids fluttering like she was going to pass out again.

'That's not what you said that day I broke six panes of glass in your greenhouse.' Lauren was relieved to see that her pathetic attempt at humour was rewarded with a half-smile. She was even more relieved to hear the sound of approaching sirens.

Within minutes the paramedics, with their usual calm efficiency, had got Elsie off the floor and on to a stretcher, reassured her that, as far as they could tell, there were no broken bones, but that a trip to the hospital was just a precaution.

Lauren stood outside with Conor and watched an ambulance drive away. Elsie, at least, looked a lot better than poor Bradley had done the day before. She was also beginning to sound more like her old self as she grumbled about how she didn't need to be taken anywhere, that it was nothing that a sticking plaster and a couple of aspirin wouldn't sort out, and no wonder the NHS was stretched to breaking point if they wasted their money forcing folks to go to hospital when they didn't want — or indeed need — to go.

'What were you doing here?' Lauren asked Conor as they stood side by side on Elsie's front path, watching the ambulance disappear down the road. 'I thought you were going to be clamped to the phone for another hour.'

'And so I will when I get back,' he said. 'But I felt like some fresh air and thought I'd bring you your bag to save you coming into the office. I was just walking past when I heard the dog barking and saw that the front door was open.'

'But Elsie never leaves her front door open, in case Dooley gets out.'

'Lucky for her she did today, then. I glanced in as I went past, the way you do, and saw her lying there at the foot of the stairs. I imagine she tripped and cracked her head on the newel post at the bottom as she went down.'

Lauren shivered. 'Seeing her lying there like that brought memories of Bradley flooding back as it must have done for you. Not that the memories had ever gone away. But you know what I mean.'

But it brought another memory back as well. Something that made her stomach lurch. Something she'd only now remembered when Conor mentioned stairs.

'You were there before me, weren't you?' she blurted out.

'How do you mean? Where?'

'Yesterday morning. You were in the office before me. I heard your footsteps coming down the stairs. But if you'd just come in, they'd be going up.'

'Sure I was there. I made no secret of the fact, and why would I? I'm often in early. More often than Bradley and that's a fact. But I didn't hear or see anything unusual, apart from the fact that Bradley's door was closed as I went past. Which meant, I assumed, that he had someone with him. And I didn't call in to wish him good morning, either. We weren't exactly on those sorts of terms.'

'You didn't mention that.'

'I wasn't aware you required a detailed account of my movements,' he said stiffly.

'And now I find you bending over

Elsie with blood all over your hands and your clothes.'

'From trying to stop the bleeding. It didn't look like a very deep wound, but, there was a lot of blood. Good Lord — ' He broke off and stared at her. 'You didn't think . . . '

'And what was it Elsie remembered when she came round just now? Was it that she remembered seeing you? You know she came to the office to see Bradley yesterday morning, don't you? But that she chickened out at the last minute? Did you see her? Or, more to the point, did she see you?'

'If I didn't know better, I'd think it was you, not Elsie, who's had the bang on the head,' he said, his eyes hot and angry.

But Lauren ignored him. She couldn't help herself. The questions kept storming through her head like a runaway train. 'Who are you, Conor? And what's a London trained accountant doing in a dead-end job in a dead-end town like Stoneford? Hardly an obvious career move for a high flier like you. And then there's the way you never talk about yourself or where you come from. Every time I ask, just trying to be friendly, you blank me like I've got the plague. In fact, before you mentioned you had sisters, the only thing I knew about you is that you don't like marmalade — '

'What?' He looked at her as if she'd just sprouted an extra head or two.

Lauren didn't think this was the time to explain how this particular nugget of gossip had come from Elsie, via his landlady, which meant that by now everyone in Stoneford knew about his aversion to marmalade.

'Well, you could be . . . ' But her runaway train had just run out of steam. And as there was no tactful way of finishing that sentence, she shrugged and gave up. Instead, she went into the house, took Dooley's lead from the hook in the kitchen and came back to see Conor standing in the doorway, glaring at her.

'Well, go on. I could be what?' he

demanded. 'A would-be murderer? Is that what you think?'

This would have been followed by a tense silence had it not been for Dooley. He took advantage of Conor's attention being totally focused on Lauren and started barking himself into a frenzy again at the sound of approaching footsteps. Lauren beat him to the gate, which she quickly shut before he could run out onto the road. But it was a close call.

'Oh Lauren, there you are,' a shrill voice called. 'Did I hear sirens? See an ambulance pulling away? Was it poor old Elsie? What happened?'

It was Sandra Wilde. She was wrapped in a fake leopard-skin coat and tottering around on four-inch heels, carrying a bag the size of a suitcase.

'She had a fall,' Lauren explained. 'Banged her head. She's been taken to hospital as a precaution.'

'That's the trouble with these old people living on their own. They're really not very safe. Some of these old houses can be death traps, you know,' Sandra said. 'They're much better off in a home, that's what I say.'

'Not in front of Elsie, I hope.' Lauren bristled on Elsie's behalf.

'But what are you doing out and about?' Sandra went on. 'I was on my way to see you. Because according to our Scott, you were at death's door earlier this morning.'

'Well, I'm not, as you can see.'

'And here was me, bringing you a little something to make you feel better.' She fished into her bag and took out a large bottle of a dark, cloudy liquid and held it up to the light. 'My best rhubarb rum. Purely medicinal, of course. Guaranteed to put the roses back in your cheeks. But it doesn't look as if you'll be needing it after all.'

Lauren gave a sigh of relief as Sandra put the bottle back in her bag. The last time Lauren had drunk Sandra's rhubarb rum, it had given her a headache for a fortnight.

'And this is — ?' Sandra turned her

236

attention to Conor. 'No, don't tell me. I never forget a face. You're the new man who works for Bradley, aren't you? Saw you in the high street a couple of weeks ago when young Lauren here almost stepped out in front of a white van. I said to our Scott, 'that girlfriend of yours needs to look where she's going,' and he said — '

'Look, I'm sorry,' Conor cut in. 'I've got to go. I've got a million things to do.'

He gave Sandra a curt nod, and Lauren a look that would have frozen boiling oil, and stalked off.

'Well, he obviously hadn't come around to cheer you up, had he?' Sandra commented in a loud voice that was aimed at Conor's back. 'Not with a face like that. Talk about if looks could kill. And — Oh. My. God.' Her hand flew to her mouth and her eyes widened as she relished the drama of the moment and milked it for all it was worth. 'You — you don't think — ?'

'Don't think what?'

'Well, for goodness sake, didn't you see his shirt?' she hissed. 'It was covered in blood. Was it him, do you think, what did for poor old Elsie? I mean, he looked like he has a temper on him, didn't he?'

'Oh no, Sandra. No. You've got it all wrong,' Lauren said quickly. 'Elsie had an accident. She must have fallen down the stairs and cracked her head on the post at the bottom. It was Conor who found her.'

'Conor, is that his name? Well, do you think it was him who attacked Bradley? After all, he hasn't been in the town five minutes and this is the first time anything like this has ever happened here in Stoneford.'

'Of course I don't think that,' Lauren said firmly. There was no way she was going to tell Sandra that that was, in fact, exactly the thought that had run through her head.

'And I must say,' Sandra went on, looking at Conor's retreating figure, 'he's got very odd taste in briefcases. I thought accountants were supposed to be ultra-conventional.'

But Lauren wasn't listening. She was too busy trying to get rid of the thought that had not only run through her head but had sat down and stayed there.

Had Conor attacked Bradley?

17

Conor was still shaking with anger as he walked away. He couldn't believe that Lauren of all people should think like that. As for the woman with her, she'd looked at him as if he'd been caught red-handed.

He looked down at his bloodstained cuffs and pushed them up under his jacket sleeves out of sight. Well, OK, maybe he couldn't blame her there. He must have looked a sight.

And then there was the way that awful woman had gone on and on about how Lauren was her son's boyfriend, making a point of it like she was warning him off. OK, he got the message. Lauren was with Scott. And sure, why should he care? Lauren thought he was a would-be serial killer who went round knocking old ladies and middle-aged accountants over the head.

She meant nothing to him. He'd known she was trouble from the first moment they'd met. He'd decided right from day one to stay well away. And he had. Except when she looked up at him and those lovely big eyes filled with tears and she did that little hiccuppy thing that made him want to put his arms around her and protect her.

No. No. Not any more. He was going to do what he'd come to Stoneford to do and then get the hell out of this place. Preferably to an island where the only inhabitants were Trappist monks. Always assuming Trappist monks were male, of course. He'd had it up to here with women.

At that moment, his phone buzzed. He snatched it up, thinking it might be Lauren phoning to say she'd got it all wrong. Some hope.

He groaned when he saw it was Niamh. He could do without any input from her at the moment, that was for sure. *Have you done this, Conor? Have you done that?* What had he done to be plagued by all these wretched women? he thought despairingly as he switched his phone off.

He turned the corner and went along the footpath that led from the row of houses on Jubilee Terrace to the Old Founders School. The building was, indeed, in a sorry state of disrepair. Elder bushes and brambles grew around it, so you almost expected to find Sleeping Beauty asleep in her castle.

He stood looking up at it. What was it about this building? Was there some connection between this building and the fact that Bradley and his unsavoury crew were buying up Jubilee Terrace? Certainly, it was a lot closer to Jubilee Terrace than he'd realised.

But why? What benefit was Jubilee Terrace or this ramshackle old building to them? The Old Founders School was in a state of near collapse, while Jubilee Terrace consisted of a row of tiny houses with even tinier gardens. If they demolished the whole terrace, they wouldn't be able to build that many houses on the land. So where was the profit in that? And from what he knew of Bradley, he didn't do anything if there wasn't a profit in it for him.

And why did the man he'd spoken to earlier have his team on standby, just waiting for the nod? The nod to do what? Was it something to do with this wretched Stag Holdings that seemed to lurk around every corner? What was going on?

As he stood in the shadow of the old building deep in thought, a boy of about thirteen with baggy jeans and a hoodie streaked past, his skateboard narrowly missing Conor's ankles.

'Nice handbag,' the boy muttered as he rattled past. 'Cool.'

And that was the moment Conor realised he was still carrying Lauren's bag. It wasn't one of these small, discreet leather handbags. That wasn't her way. It was a big, bold look-at-me thing in an eye-watering shade of pink with huge white daisies all over it. No wonder the kid had sniggered. It looked quite ludicrous against his sombre navy pin-striped suit.

How come he still had it? What was he thinking of? Why hadn't he given it back to Lauren? Goodness knew he'd had all the time in the world to do so as they'd waited for the paramedics to do their thing. Then he remembered how as he'd knelt down to help Elsie, he'd slung it across his body and pushed it round to his back, rather than risk getting Elsie's blood on it.

Great. Now Lauren thought him not only responsible for two violent assaults, one of which was on an elderly lady, but she also had him marked down as a handbag snatcher.

He sighed, took the bag from his shoulder and made his way back to Jubilee Terrace.

★   ★   ★

'Well, I can't stand here talking all day,' Sandra Wilde said. 'I need to get back to the salon. I only popped out to drop my rhubarb rum in for you during my break. I'll see you around, Lauren.'

Lauren was relieved to see Sandra and the rhubarb rum go. But she couldn't stop herself from wishing that Conor hadn't.

She should have been glad, relieved even, when he stormed off, but she wasn't. Instead she wanted to run after him and tell him she was sorry, that she'd been mistaken. And yet, everything fitted. He *was* there yesterday when Bradley was attacked. And again today. And she only had his word for it that Elsie's door was open.

But he'd been so brilliant yesterday, so kind and gentle with her when she was upset, so cool and calm. Would he have been like that if he'd just whacked Bradley over the head? And yes, he had been standoffish before, but that didn't make him a would-be murderer, surely?

Lauren had the feeling she'd got it all wrong. Or, she asked herself, was it that she *wanted* to be wrong? Could it be that she didn't want it to be him because she had what Elsie called 'a touch of the emotionals' for him?

She whirled round as she heard footsteps coming up the path. Her face turned scarlet and her heart began to thud. He'd come back.

'Conor, I — '

'Here.' He held her bag as if it was contaminated with something unspeakable. 'I won't inflict my murderous presence on you any longer. And please feel free to share your suspicions with the police. Or indeed anyone else who you think might be interested. Although the police already know my movements yesterday morning. So sorry to disappoint you.'

'No. Conor, please don't go,' she cried, clutching her bag to her chest as if it was a lifebelt and she'd just jumped off the *Titanic*. 'Of course I don't think that. It's just — everything is such a mess. I'm not thinking straight. I didn't sleep last night for worrying. And I've got to get into the office today, otherwise I'll be locked up for years knitting mailbags. And Dad's that rubbish at cooking, he'll probably starve . . . ' Lauren hardly ever cried. But ever since yesterday, big fat tears had been hanging around just behind her eyes, waiting for any excuse to spill over.

'What are you on about now?' With the gentlest touch, he wiped away a runaway tear, sending tingles through her entire nervous system. 'You're still suffering from shock, so you are. You should be home. Come here.'

He put his arm around her, his crisp cotton shirt (it was only his cuffs that were blood-spattered) blessedly cool against her burning cheeks.

What's wrong with me? she thought in despair. *One minute I have him tagged as the villain, the next I'm trying to think of a reason to stay wrapped in his arms for the rest of my life.*

'Sorry. I don't normally cry.' Reluctantly she pulled away, and before she could stop herself, was telling him everything. 'I didn't mean you . . . it's just . . . I don't know what to do. I've done something really, really stupid.'

She put her hand in her pocket and took out the copper shield. 'Yesterday morning I found this on the floor of Bradley's office, and I thought it was my mother's. Although I had no idea how it had got there. I don't even remember taking it, but of course I must have done. Then when I got home, I went to put it back in her jewellery box, and it was still there. I mean, hers was still there. This — this must belong to Bradley, or someone.'

'Ah yes.' He nodded as he took the shield and examined it closely. 'Your mother was a Stag.'

Under normal circumstances, Lauren would have been unable to resist chirping that her mother, being the female of the species, was technically a hind. But her sense of humour, like the rest of her senses, had deserted her.

'I must have picked it up when I almost broke my toe on Bradley's doorstop.' She shuddered as the very mention of the thing brought the memories flooding back and sent her imagination into overdrive. She had a vivid mental image of someone raising it high above Bradley's head and bringing it crashing down.

'Hey, it's OK. It's OK.' He put his arm around her again and held her close. 'Look, I'll probably get marched off to jail for this, but would you like me to return it for you? I'm about to hand over the file on Stag Holdings to the police. I could always say I found it in there.'

Stag Holdings? Wasn't that the company Bradley wanted her to work on? But why would the police be interested in that? Or, come to that, why would Conor?

'You can trust me, you know,' he said softly when she didn't answer. 'And, if it'll help, I know what Elsie was trying to say just now when she was coming round. She recognised me. When I found her, just before you got here, she said,

'You're Dora's grandson, aren't you?''

'Dora?'

'Did you know Dora Maguire?'

'The name rings a bell. Not sure why, though.'

'She was my grandmother. She lived a couple of doors down from Elsie until her death six months ago. She was Stoneford born and bred, but met my grandfather and went to live in Ireland. When he died, she left Ireland to come back home, as she always called it. Elsie recognised me from Granny Maguire's funeral.'

'Oh, right. I see.' A wave of relief washed over her.

'I'd just broken up with my girl-friend — '

A second wave washed over Lauren. This time, it was one of cautious optimism. Did he say he'd just broken up with his girlfriend? 'And you don't care for marmalade,' she murmured, rather than say what was really on her mind.

He drew away and frowned at her.

'What's this about me and marmalade?'

'Don't ask. Carry on with what you were saying. You'd just what?'

'Broken up with my girlfriend (and it was nothing to do with marmalade, I promise) and I needed a change of scenery. I didn't fancy going back to Ireland where my mother and sisters would plague the life out of me to find a good Irish woman and settle down. Then somebody told me about the job going at Northcott and Company and said I ought to go for it. So I thought maybe Stoneford would be as good a place as any to hunker down while I worked out what the hell I was going to do with the rest of my life.'

Something went ping inside Lauren's head. A true lightbulb moment. She didn't know how Elsie had fallen. She didn't know who had attacked Bradley. And she had absolutely no idea why stags kept rearing their heads — or should that be antlers? — at every turn. But she knew, with blinding certainty, that Conor was telling the truth.

'I'm sorry I said all those stupid things,' she murmured.

'And I'm sorry I've been so standoffish,' he said. 'I made an assumption about you that was completely wrong.'

'What assumption?'

'The day before your interview, I came across the file for Stag Holdings. As I went to put it away, the words 'Jubilee Terrace' caught my eye, being Granny Maguire's old address. I carried on reading and realised that Bradley wasn't just lazy and incompetent as I'd thought — he'd hardly done a day's work since I joined the company and I spent most of my time covering up his errors — but something much more serious.'

'Such as?'

He hesitated. 'I can't tell you the full story. Not yet. I've found out a few things while I've had the office to myself, and there's stuff I need to check out first.'

'But what's all this got to do with me?' she asked.

'I thought you were L. E. Chapman.'

'I am. You know that.'

'No. I thought you were one of the Stag shareholders involved in Bradley's iffy property deals up to your neck.'

Lauren disentangled herself from his arms. Suddenly, she felt cold. Very cold. 'And now?' she asked quietly.

'Well, now I don't. Obviously.' He looked puzzled.

'And yet you're prepared to believe that my mother was,' she snapped. 'Is that what you're going to tell the police?'

'Well, yes, I suppose. Always assuming she was.'

'You've no right to make such an assumption,' she said as she turned to walk away. 'My mother would never in a million years do anything underhanded. Which is more than I can say for you, Conor Maguire.'

As an exit line, though, it would have worked a lot better if she hadn't forgotten that she was still holding Dooley, as dog and lead became hopelessly tangled around the gatepost.

253

18

'My husband's going to be a vegetable?' Isobel stared at the white-haired man on the other side of the desk. She had this wild urge to giggle and say something about Bradley always having been a bit of an old turnip. But she checked herself. She sat up straighter and forced herself to concentrate on his voice, which seemed to be coming at her from a long way away.

The phone call from the hospital had been because Mr Murchison, the surgeon who had operated on Bradley, would be doing his rounds that morning and wished to speak to Isobel. She'd driven all the way to the hospital in a state of high anxiety, only to be told when she got there that he had no definite news, good or bad, but merely wanted to keep her in the picture.

Relief had made her go a little

lightheaded, and now the whole scene had taken on a surreal quality, from the picture of Jemima Puddleduck on the wall alongside a poster about washing your hands, to the fact that Mr Murchison had a halo of white fluffy hair and bristly eyebrows that seemed to have a life of their own, and looked more like Father Christmas than a brain surgeon. Not that she'd met that many brain surgeons, of course. But she was sure most of them didn't look like Father Christmas.

She put her lightheadedness down to too much wine last night and not enough sleep. That and the overwhelming sense of relief on learning that Bradley was, in fact, still alive. Although apparently still unconscious. But now she was being warned that he was going to be a vegetable? Suddenly she didn't feel like making turnip jokes anymore. Suddenly it didn't seem very funny at all. Just sad and a bit scary.

Mr Murchison's eyebrows jerked together like two furry caterpillars squaring up for a fight. He sighed, steepled his long thin fingers in front of him, and spoke in a voice full of exaggerated patience as if he really was Father Christmas and was having to explain to a particularly overexcited child why they had to wait six more sleeps until Christmas day.

'You know, I really wish people wouldn't use that expression,' he said wearily. 'No, my dear, I didn't for one moment mean that your husband is going to be a vegetable. At this stage of the process, a vegetative state simply means, in layman's terms, that your husband is in a coma. And I apologise if my use of the word 'vegetative state', which is merely a technical term, alarmed you.'

'Oh, right. I see. Thank you,' she murmured.

'To be honest, Mrs Northcott, the longer he remains in that state — in the short term, at least — the better, because it gives a chance for the swelling in his brain to go down naturally. Much the preferred option.'

'Yes, of course.' She scrabbled around in her mind for something more intelligent to say. Preferably something that didn't involve vegetables. 'How long is he going to be in this veg — I mean, coma?' she asked.

His halo of white curls danced as he shook his head. 'That, I'm afraid, I can't tell you. There's still so much about brain injury that we simply don't know. It could be days, it could be weeks. It's impossible to predict. I'm sorry. But I am hopeful; let's say that, shall we? Hopeful.' His little blue eyes twinkled in a very Father Christmassy way as he smiled at her.

'Can he hear me?' Isobel asked.

Once again, he shook his white curls. 'Who knows, my dear. There have been many instances when people who have woken from a coma say they remember things being said to them, or favourite music being played, that sort of thing. Does your husband have any favourite music? Any special tune that might evoke memories? It won't do any harm, that's for sure. But it may help. You never know.'

Isobel made her way to Bradley's ward and drew a blue plastic chair closer to his bed. She leaned towards him and began to speak in a low soft tone.

'They say it'll help if I talk to you, Bradley,' she began, her mouth barely inches away from his left ear. 'So here goes. I used to love you, you know, I really did. Or I thought it was love. And I tried to be a good wife to you. But you weren't a good husband to me. In so many ways. Do you know the thing I've always disliked about you? It's the way you put me down, how you tell me and others how stupid I am. Because I'm not stupid, you know. And then there's that really annoying thing you do . . . '

She went on and on and on. Talking to him for hours. Because for the first time since she'd known him, she could actually get to the end of a sentence without him cutting across, telling her not to make a show of herself and to be quiet. For the first time, she was able to tell him about the things she was interested in, about the opinions she had, about her hopes and dreams. Well, some of them at least. She didn't think this was either the time or the place to mention Antonio.

At last she was done. She leaned across and said goodbye, then made her way out of the ward.

The nurse at the desk gave her a smile of approval. 'I'm sure talking to him like that helps him, Mrs Bradley.'

'I do hope so, Nurse,' Isobel said. 'I'll be back again tomorrow.'

Her steps were lighter as she walked down the long hospital corridors. She didn't know if her talking was helping Bradley. But it was sure helping her.

* * *

Conor was still fuming when he got back to the office. One minute Lauren was looking at him like she fancied him, and the next she was shrinking away like he was the devil himself. What was she up to? He put his hand in his pocket to find the office keys when his fingers caught on the sharp edges of the little badge. What was that all that about? And what had she been thinking of, removing it from a crime scene?

He took it out and examined it. It was obviously handmade. The copper had tarnished over the years, but the shape of a stag's head engraved on it still stood out. Simple but effective. A badge of office. Such an innocent-looking thing for such a corrupt organisation, if his suspicions were correct.

He went up in to Bradley's office, trying not to look at the stain that marred the smooth leather top of his very grand desk. 'Where is it, Bradley?' he muttered to the empty room. 'Where have you hidden the Stag Holdings file?'

Because although he'd sounded very

smart and sure of himself when he'd talked about handing the file over to the police, the truth was that he'd only said it to impress Lauren. The fact was, he couldn't find it anywhere, and was beginning to think that Bradley had destroyed it after all. And then, where would his evidence be?

He turned his phone back on, and as he did so, it rang. This time he answered it. 'Hi, Niamh,' he said wearily. 'And before you ask, no I haven't got any further.'

'So what have you been doing with yourself, Conor Maguire? Don't tell me, you've met this woman — '

'Yes. I mean, no.' How did she do this, this big sister of his? How did she read his mind, even when the Irish Sea and then some separated them? 'There's been a bit of a development. Bradley Northcott was attacked in his office yesterday and is in a coma.'

There was a small shocked silence on the other end. But with Niamh, silence was one of those things that never lasted very long.

'Was it anything to do with all these shenanigans about Jubilee Terrace?' she asked. 'Because if that's the case, Conor, you'd better be careful about going around asking questions. I told you they weren't very nice people, didn't I?'

'No you didn't. You told me to get in there, apply for the job and see what was going on. And I'm beginning to find out. It seems a lot of the other tenants have been given notices to quit in the last month or so, including an old lady who I found in a heap at the bottom of her stairs this morning.'

'Then you just stop whatever it is you're doing and get out of that place at once,' Niamh said in her firm I-will-not-be-argued-with voice. 'I know I asked you to find out what had happened to Granny Maguire's deposit and everything, but she wouldn't want you to be putting yourself into danger on her account.'

When she'd first 'suggested' it, not long after the funeral, Conor merely thought she'd been watching too many episodes of *Hustle*. But he'd been at a loose end, so he went along with it. He had, after all, nothing better to do and nowhere better to go. And, of course, he felt he owned Granny Maguire. But now Niamh was telling him to get out of Stoneford just when he was beginning to get somewhere? No way.

'I've started so I'll finish,' he murmured. 'Look, I'll catch you later, OK? And thanks for worrying about me, but there really is no need, I promise you.'

He ended the call and started to look through Bradley's excessively neat desk drawers. Again, his phone rang. He almost didn't answer it, thinking it was Niamh calling back to give him more instructions. But he changed his mind when he saw who the caller was.

'Mrs Northcott,' he said. 'How's your husband?'

'No change, Conor,' she said. 'And like I told you before, please call me Isobel.'

'OK. So, what can I do for you, Isobel?'

'I rather think it might be what I can do for you,' she said, and he thought she sounded a little out of breath, as if she'd just run up the stairs.

'In what way?' he prompted when it looked as if she wasn't going to continue.

'Yesterday you asked me about a company called Stag Holdings. Are you still interested in it?'

Conor froze, his heart thumping so loud he was afraid she'd hear. 'I certainly am. Do you know anything about it?'

'I know Bradley shuts up if I or anyone else mention it.'

'Do you know why?'

'No. I never really understood all that financial stuff, if you must know. But I've just found a file. It was in Bradley's bedside cabinet, pushed right to the back. I was looking for some CDs and things to take into hospital for him. Mr Murchison said they might help him wake up.'

'What's in the file? Did you read it?'

'I couldn't make head or tail of it. Just a load of stuff about shares and things. But you might. Would you like it?'

19

By the time Lauren had separated Dooley and his lead from the gatepost, Conor was long gone.

'And good riddance too,' Lauren muttered, still angry with Conor, but even angrier with herself for falling for him. 'Come on, Dooley. Let's go to the park, shall we? And no barking at squirrels or litter bins. Or anything else, come to that. I'm really not in the mood for your nonsense today.'

As she went through the ornate wrought-iron gates at the park entrance (a gift to the people of Stoneford from some long-gone Victorian mill owner who refused to pay his workers a living wage but lavished money on a fancy pair of gates that were never closed), Dooley gave that low growl that signified he was about to kick off.

'Stop it,' Lauren said in what she

thought was a voice of firm authority, the way Conor had earlier. 'It's just a man wearing a hat. There's nothing wrong with people wearing hats. He's a runner. It probably keeps the rain or maybe the sweat — '

She stopped so abruptly that Dooley, who was some way in front, was jerked so hard against the lead that he almost fell over. Certainly it cut off him off mid-bark. Which was a result, even if it had been unintended.

He gave her a reproachful, look but Lauren was too stunned to apologise. She was still trying to pin down that elusive feeling that she was on the verge of remembering something significant.

And then it came to her. It was yesterday morning. She was on her way into the office, worried she might be late. The rain was lashing down, flattening bushes and making tiny waterfalls as it rushed into the overflowing gutters. And there in the middle of all that rain, moving at a steady pace and making no attempt to avoid the puddles, was a runner in shorts, vest — and a hat. Not the runner here in the park, of course. He was wearing baggy tracksuit bottoms and a sweat-stained T-shirt. Red of face and short of breath. The man she'd seen yesterday was slender and dark and moved with an easy, fluid grace.

She'd told the police she'd seen no one that morning (she didn't think they needed to know about Elsie) — and yet, of course, she had seen someone. As she'd turned the corner into the road, he'd been coming past Bradley's office. He might even have been coming out of Bradley's office, for all she knew. She'd had her head bent low against the driving rain at the time, but remembered exchanging a rueful smile with him as they passed each other.

Should she tell the police what she'd remembered? Yes, of course she should. But first, she wanted to talk it through with Conor.

'Come on, Dooley,' she called as they left the park. 'You can come back and

268

bark at the litter bins later, I promise.'

She took a short cut through the car park, and as she did so, she looked up to see Conor coming towards her. She was so pleased to see him — seemingly she only had to think of him and there he was — that she had a wild urge to run towards him in one of those Cathy and Heathcliff moments, as if they were in the middle of the Yorkshire moors instead of Stoneford Long Stay Car Park.

'You must be psychic,' she said. 'I was just coming to see you.'

'I'm sorry, but I've got to be somewhere,' he said, which completely ruined her Cathy and Heathcliff fantasy, which was probably no bad thing considering how things turned out for them. 'I'm in a bit of a hurry. Can it wait?'

'I just wanted to tell you that I remembered seeing a runner yesterday morning. He was right by Bradley's office. Do you think I should tell the police?'

'A runner, you say?' He pressed his car key, and a silver grey BMW gave an answering chirrup. 'Can you describe him?'

'It was only a brief glimpse because of the rain. He was good-looking in a Mediterranean sort of way. Slim, dark and tanned, about five ten, with well-developed muscles. He looked pretty fit from the way he moved.'

'For someone who only got a brief glance, you sure noticed a lot of detail.' He gave her a quick scowl, then his face cleared. 'Hang on a minute. I think I might have seen the same guy. Was he wearing a dark blue running vest and shorts and a black baseball cap?'

'That's him. Did you see him too? Where?'

'Not anywhere near the office. But here. He was running across the car park when I was parking the car. I assumed he'd come out of here. In fact, I — ' He broke off.

'In fact, you what?' she asked, but he shook his head.

'In fact, I've got to go,' he said. 'I need to see someone. It's pretty urgent. But I'll call you when I get back. Perhaps we could have a drink together? There's something I want to talk through with you. Something I need to tell you.'

'What about?'

He glanced at his watch. 'I really don't have time. But I'll tell you everything later, I promise. Well, everything I know. Meanwhile, how about you tell me something?'

'How does that work?' Lauren demanded. 'You're in too much of a hurry to answer my questions, yet you expect me to answer yours. Well I'm very sorry, Conor Maguire, but it so happens I'm in a rush too, as it happens. Come on, Dooley.' She turned, gave Dooley a tug on the lead, and stalked off.

'Lauren,' he called, 'I think I know what happened. With your mother and everything. But I just need a little bit more evidence before I go around accusing anyone.'

'Charming! And yet you didn't mind

accusing my mother. She — '

'Did Bradley get you to sign anything?' he cut in. 'You said something a while back about how he was going to train you up as a company secretary.'

'And you said I wasn't up to the job,' she retorted.

'No, that was what Bradley *said* I said. I didn't know anything about it. And you haven't answered my question. Did Bradley get you to sign anything?'

'No. But he was going to. That was why I was coming in early yesterday. He said it was just a few simple forms, very boring. He said I didn't even need to read them. But — '

'I'll catch you later,' he said and sprinted for his car — leaving Lauren trying to convince the parking attendant that Dooley wasn't a dangerous dog who needed to be carted off to the pound, but had simply taken a dislike to his hat.

★   ★   ★

Isobel moved the remnants of her breakfast to one side and placed the file on the kitchen table. Conor snatched it up.

'What are you looking for?' she asked as he leafed eagerly through the papers. 'I must say, I had a quick look through while I was waiting for you, but it all seemed quite straightforward and boring.'

'Is this all there is?'

'Yes, as far as I know.'

'Does Bradley have any more papers lying around the house? His study, maybe?'

She shook her head. 'It's very unlike him to bring his work home at all. So is this not any use to you?'

She was disappointed. She'd been so sure there was something iffy about this folder — why else would Bradley go to the trouble of finding it? — and that Conor was going to discover what it was he'd been up to. How lovely if, when he finally did come around, there was a fraud charge waiting for him.

'I'm not sure.' Conor frowned as he

studied the papers. 'Although I'm beginning to get an idea of what's going on here. What do you know about Stag Holdings?'

She chewed her thumbnail and tried to remember. 'It was all a long time ago now. But I was working for Bradley at the time — this was before we were married, you understand. I do remember some of it. There was a group of traders in the town who got all upset because there was a rumour of a supermarket opening up just off the high street and they wanted to stop it. Said it would kill the high street. Which, of course, is exactly what did happen when the council allowed the out-of-town development a couple of years back. So it was all for nothing really, when you think about it.'

'And Stag Holdings?'

'Oh that was what they called themselves. The Stags. I don't know where the Holdings bit came from. Bradley said it was all a bit silly and used to poke fun of them behind their backs.

But I thought it was quite sweet that they'd formed this little club to fight the big bully boys from the supermarket. Sort of a David and Goliath thing. Let me see, they called it something like Stoneford Traders Action Group, or some-such. I can't remember. Anyway, it spelt out S-T-A-G, and someone made them each a little badge with a stag's head on it. And they had meetings and so on. I liked them.'

'Well, they must have succeeded, as there's no supermarket in the high street,' Conor said. 'It's not easy, seeing off a supermarket. How did they do it? Do you know?'

She shook her head. 'I'm afraid not. But like I said, that was years ago, and most of the people involved aren't around anymore. Some have moved away, some retired, some even died. It might have escaped your notice, but there aren't too many traders left in Stoneford any-more, not if you take the mobile phone and charity shops out of the equation. I'm sorry I can't be any more help.'

'You've been great.' Conor gave her a warm smile. 'You're looking a bit better today, Mrs — '

'Isobel. How many times do I have to remind you?'

'Sorry, Isobel. Does that mean the news about Mr Northcott is better?'

'It's still too early to say, Conor. But the consultant I spoke to yesterday was cautiously optimistic. Although as to whether he'll have any memory of who attacked him, that's another matter.'

'I'll keep my fingers crossed for him,' he said. 'And when he does come round, be sure to tell him that he's not to fret about getting back to the office, that I'm managing things perfectly well in his absence.'

I'll bet you are, Isobel thought, but restrained herself. But Conor was right about one thing. She was indeed feeling a lot more positive this morning. More positive than she'd done for ages. Talking to Bradley in his hospital bed yesterday had released something within her. It was as if all the self-doubts and lack of confidence that had built up slowly over the years she'd been married had suddenly melted away. They said it was good to talk, didn't they? And it was even better to talk when the other party had no option but to listen.

In her room upstairs were two suitcases she was in the process of packing. As soon as she learned Bradley was out of danger, she'd be on her way. She wanted nothing from him. Not anymore. He could have his divorce and she wouldn't ask him for a penny. That way, things would go through quicker. She'd already been in contact with her friend Jo from way back, who'd bought a hotel in Dorset a few years ago and had offered her a job several times and somewhere to live.

'The day you wake up, Isobel, and see the man you married for the control freak he really is,' she'd said, 'I'll be here for you. You'll make a brilliant front-of-house person, I've always said that. The guests will love you.'

Well, she had woken up. And as soon

as Bradley did the same, she'd be off. But in the meantime . . . She stood up and showed Conor to the door. 'Thank you so much for coming round,' she said. 'I hope you find what you're looking for. Now, I don't want to rush you, but I have to be somewhere.'

'Of course. You'll be wanting to get to the hospital.'

Oh no she wasn't. But Conor didn't need to know that. She *was* going to the hospital. Just not straightaway. First of all, she had an appointment. With Antonio.

'I'll be off, then.' Conor turned on the doorstep. 'Oh, by the way, that man I saw you with at the country club the other day . . . '

Isobel's heart skipped a beat. She'd forgotten that Conor had seen her and Antonio together. What did he want now? 'Yes?' she kept her voice cool. 'His name's Antonio. He's my personal trainer. All perfectly aboveboard, you know.'

He looked embarrassed. 'Oh, dear

heaven, I didn't mean to imply — ' he began.

'Well, what about him?' she cut in.

'It — it's just I wondered what you knew about him. Because he was seen hanging around Bradley's office at the time of the attack. Just thought it was a bit weird, that's all.'

With an effort of will she had no idea she possessed, Isobel kept her expression bland, her voice low, with just the right amount of vagueness. 'Who knows?' she said carelessly.

But she didn't start breathing again until she heard Conor's car start up and drive away. 'Oh Antonio, Antonio,' she whispered. 'What have you done?'

Isobel's feel-good factor had suddenly evaporated faster than Cinderella's sequins after midnight.

20

The bar of the Nag's Head was empty apart from two elderly men who were playing a noisy game of dominos on the table nearest the fire. Lauren was wondering if this was such a wise choice of venue as she and Dooley followed Conor in. It was one of the few public buildings in Stoneford that Dooley hadn't got himself banned from, but that was only because it was the first time he'd been in here. It was only a matter of time before someone wearing a hat came in and set him off again.

'It's quiet in here, Mike,' Lauren commented when they got to the bar.

'Apart from those two,' he said with weary resignation. 'You wouldn't think dominos could rouse such passion, would you?'

'You should hear my sisters playing

Scrabble,' Conor said.

'So where's Keri today?' Lauren asked.

'She stayed in Bristol with one of her mates who's got a flat there,' Mike said as he poured Conor's pint. 'They went clubbing last night, apparently. I tell you, I pay that woman too much if she can afford that. *I* can't.'

Lauren grinned. 'Can't quite picture you as part of the Bristol club scene, Mike. No disrespect intended.'

He grinned back. 'You eating?'

'Yes,' said Conor while Lauren said 'No' at the same time.

'The kitchen's not up and running, but I can do you a sandwich.'

Lauren suddenly realised that for the first time since finding Bradley, she was hungry. Ravenous, in fact. 'Well?' Lauren asked, the second Mike was out of the bar. 'What was this big thing you were going to tell me?'

'First things first. How's Elsie? Have you heard?'

'I managed to get hold of Tom

— that's her son — and he's on his way in to see her right now. Says he'll ring me when he has any news. You said you were going to explain. So go on, explain away.'

'That little badge you gave me, the one with the stag's head on — '

Lauren's heart skipped a beat. 'Have you been to the police with it? Was that where you were rushing off to? To shop me?'

'No, of course not. If you must know, I went to see Isobel.'

'Isobel?' She looked down at Dooley, who had at last curled up at her feet. She didn't want Conor to see the flash of jealousy that must have been written all over her face.

'Mrs Northcott.'

'I didn't realise you and the boss's wife were on first-name terms.' She knew she was sounding waspish and petulant but couldn't help herself. She put it down to lack of food.

'We're not. Look, do you want to hear this or not? Only I've got a million and one other things to be getting on with.'

'Sorry,' she muttered, although she felt anything but. 'Go on.'

'What do you remember about a group that called themselves the Stags?' he asked.

'Nothing,' she said.

'But I do,' said Mike as he came across with two plates of beef sand-wiches. 'I was one of them.'

'You were?' Lauren said. 'Who else?'

'Just about everyone in the town. The butcher, the baker and the candlestick maker. It stood for Stoneford Traders Action Group, and it was all your mother's idea. In fact, she made us — '

'A little copper badge with a stag's head on it,' she said. 'I remember that for sure, but I don't remember anything else.'

'It was all a long time ago now,' he said. 'Your mother had all sorts of wonderful ideas to breathe life into this town. She was a power house of energy, and could get anyone to do anything.

Anyway, she persuaded almost everyone in the town to buy a share in the Old Founders School at the back of Jubilee Terrace. That was the bit of land the developers were interested in buying, you see. They were going to demolish it. But your mother had this thing about turning it into a community centre. She would have, too, if — ' He broke off and looked uncomfortable.

'If she'd lived,' Lauren finished the sentence for him. 'You know, I do remember that now. But I was so caught up in school exams and everything, I didn't really take that much notice.'

'But when I was asking about the building in the bar the other night,' Conor said, 'you didn't say anything about owning a share in it.'

Mike scratched the back of his neck and sighed. 'That's because I don't anymore. To be honest, I feel a bit of a fool about the whole thing. And I didn't fancy telling you that in front of Keri. She already thinks her old man is the biggest idiot in the world without giving her any more ammunition.'

'What happened?' Lauren asked gently.

'It was that Bradley Northcott. Came up with some scare story about how the building was about to have a preservation order slapped on it and how each shareholder was going to have to find goodness knows how much to comply with the regulations.'

'So you sold your share to Bradley?'

'No, not him. To this company he set up. He said that way no one would be able to trace the original owners and we wouldn't be landed with a bill for thousands. I can hardly afford to keep this place open, least of all a building that's falling down. I couldn't wait to sign my share away, even though I never got a penny for it.'

'And who were the other shareholders? Do you remember?'

'Well, there was your mother, of course. Of the original members, I'm probably the only one who's still around. All the others have retired or moved away. Apart from Sandra Wilde, of course. And Den Uppington.'

'And did they sell their shares to this company that Bradley set up?'

'I'm pretty sure they did. I remember talking to both of them at the time and we all agreed it was for the best. Glad to be shot of the whole thing, to be honest. Only now I think about it, and have been talking to people, it seems we were a bit foolish to hand over our shares without proper legal advice. If your mother had still been around, Lauren, she'd have stood up to Bradley and his nonsense. Still, all water under the bridge now, I suppose. But it taught me a lesson, I can tell you.'

At that moment, two more elderly men came in to join the dominos grudge match and he hurried off to serve them, leaving Lauren and Conor to get on with their sandwiches under Dooley's hawk-like supervision.

'That Bradley!' Lauren exclaimed. 'I could kill him — ' She broke off as she realised what she'd just said. 'Oh my God, I didn't mean it like that.'

'I know what you meant,' Conor said grimly. 'He conned my Granny Maguire and all. That's why I came to Stoneford in the first place.'

'How do you mean?'

Conor took a long pull at his drink. 'After Granny Maguire died, we found out that she'd been tricked out of her money by some unscrupulous landlord who'd promised her she could buy number four Jubilee Terrace and had taken a not insubstantial deposit from her.'

'And she moved back to Stoneford after your grandfather died,' Lauren said. 'Yes, you told me.'

Conor nodded. 'When he died she was, as I said, keen to come back here. So keen that she wasn't too careful about checking out the legal stuff.'

'And she lived two doors down from Elsie, didn't she? I didn't really know her, but she wasn't here very long, was she?'

His face darkened. 'No. We think the stress of losing her money like that brought on the stroke that killed her. Something I feel really guilty about now.'

'In what way is it your fault?'

He shrugged. 'I had a lot of personal stuff going on in my life at the time. Things weren't working out between me and my girlfriend. Maybe if I'd had my head on straighter, I'd have insisted on checking things out for her. Anyway, this guy 'very kindly' allowed her to move in as a tenant while the 'legal stuff', as he put it, was sorted out.'

Lauren finished the last of the beef sandwich, slipped Dooley a crust and wiped her hands. 'So what happened?'

'In the end, what she'd thought was an agreement to buy had been nothing more than a tenancy agreement with more holes in it than a lace curtain. And like Mike here, she'd been so embarrassed about being conned that it wasn't until after she died that the whole sad story came out.'

'Oh Conor, the poor soul. That's terrible. So that's why you've come here?'

He nodded. 'Niamh — she's the bossiest of my bossy sisters — suggested, when she heard I was giving up my job in London, that I apply for the vacancy she'd heard was going at Northcott and Company. Don't ask me how she knew. I suspect my sister is a witch.'

'And if she is, what does that make you then?' Lauren asked with a laugh. But before he could answer, her phone rang. She was about to turn it off when she saw the caller was Elsie's son, Tom.

'How is she?' she asked.

'She's fine. But they're keeping her in overnight, just in case.'

There was something about his voice that made Lauren uneasy. 'What's wrong?' she asked. 'Did she tell you what happened?'

'Sort of. She started to and then she got a bit — well, a bit weird. She said something about having it out with him

289

— whoever 'he' is. And then went on about jeans. And when I said I didn't know she even had a pair of jeans, she asked me if my ears needed syringing again, and started on about when I was six and had grommets put in my ears.' He gave a long sigh. 'I have to say, I'm more than a little worried about her. She's very confused. But they're hoping that after a good night's sleep, she'll be back to her old self again.'

Something went ping inside Lauren's head. She ended the call with Tom and turned back to Conor. 'Did your grandmother happen to say who owned the house in Jubilee Terrace?'

'She did. It was that weird greengrocer you used to work for.'

'Den Uppington?'

Conor nodded. 'He and Bradley are as thick as thieves. That was why when you started work at the office, I thought you were in on it as well.'

'Well, I wasn't.'

'I know that now.'

'So what made you change your

290

mind?' she asked. 'Your were quick enough to have me tried and convicted before.'

He fidgeted in his chair. 'I just know, that's all. Did you say Elsie was at the office that morning? As well as the mysterious runner — who, incidentally, I've managed to identify.'

It was a pretty abrupt change of subject, but she let it go. For now. 'Elsie was there because she was going to have it out with Bradley, as he'd given her notice to quit her house.'

'She must have been pretty upset.'

'She was. Of course.' She glared at him. 'You surely don't think she bashed Bradley over the head. What about this mysterious runner? Who was he? Do you think he could have done it?'

'Can't think why he would. But yes, I know who he is. He works at Stoneford Manor Country Club. One of their fitness instructors.'

She raised an eyebrow. 'I wouldn't have had you down as a gym bunny, Conor.'

'I'm not. But Isobel Northcott is.'

'Isobel Northcott?' She leaned towards him. 'You don't think — '

'I'll tell you what I think. That you read too many murder mysteries.'

'I do not.' She stood up. 'Well, thanks for the sandwiches, but I've got things to do.'

'Like what? I thought you could come with me to see Elsie. See if we can get her to tell us a bit more about this notice to quit, and if she remembers anything about the accident.'

'No, I'll see her later. Give her my love, won't you?'

'So what are you going to do?'

'I'm going to have a go at Den Uppington, the rat. Tell him exactly what I think of him going around conning little old ladies.'

'Don't do that, Lauren. You never know, he could be the attacker.'

Lauren gave a shout of laughter that startled Dooley awake, and he let off a furious volley of barks that earned reproving stares and tuts from the noisy domino players.

'Den? You've got to be kidding. He couldn't hurt a fly. Literally. He was always calling on me to deal with the wasps and flies that hung around his rotten fruit and veg.'

'You don't know what a person is capable of.'

'I know what Den is capable of,' she snorted. 'Not a lot.'

'OK, then. How about we go and see him together?'

'No. You go and see Elsie. I'll take Dooley for a walk. We didn't have much time in the park earlier.'

He looked at her closely, his eyes narrowed with suspicion.

'And you promise you won't do anything silly like going to see Den Uppington on your own?'

'OK.'

'We'll meet back here at 5 o'clock and go and see him together. Promise?'

'I promise,' she said as she bent down to untie Dooley's lead from the chair leg. 'Come on, Dooley. Let's see if we can find any more litter bins for you to bark at.'

If Conor had been watching a little more closely, he'd have seen that Lauren's fingers were tightly crossed as she said 'I promise'.

And everyone knows promises don't count if you have your fingers crossed when you make them.

21

'Is-so-bella.' Antonio came out into Reception to greet her. He looked as handsome as ever, his smile as if it was meant for her alone. 'You are not changed. You are not well? Not do training today?'

'No, Antonio. Not today. But I do need to see you. To speak to you. Is there somewhere we can go? Somewhere private?'

He looked puzzled. She turned towards the coffee shop and saw it was empty apart from a group of sleek track-suited women in one corner. She chose a table as far away from them as possible and sat down. Antonio followed her.

'You want a coffee?' he asked. 'Or some of my favourite green juice? Very good to you?'

Isobel shuddered at the memory of the time she'd tried it. It seemed so long ago that it was as if it had happened to another person. Which, in a way, she had been. Another person foolish enough to imagine herself in love with a handsome boy. What had she been thinking? She blushed at the memory.

'No, I don't want anything to drink. Antonio, sit down please. There's something I have to ask you. You know that morning I saw you running in the rain?'

'You saw me?'

'Yes. I was early and was in here having a coffee and I saw you. I — I wondered where you'd been.'

'I was running.'

'Yes, but . . . ' She took a deep breath. 'Did you go along Sefton Street? That's the one I told you about. Where my husband has his office. You asked me about him, remember?'

'Your husband. A bad man to hurt you. Yes, I did. I was hoping to see him.'

'And did you? Did you . . . ' This was hard. So much harder than she'd expected. How she wished she'd thought more carefully about what she was going to say. Nothing for it. Just come out with it. 'Did you attack my husband? Did you hurt him? Because — because if you did, I'll tell the police that you were with me at the time.'

'Why would you do that? And why would I be with you at this time of the morning?'

At first, he looked more confused than ever. Then she saw the very moment he realised what she was talking about.

'You think I hurt him?' he said. 'But why would I do such a thing?'

'Because . . . because you thought that was what I wanted you to do.'

'I'm sorry, I don't understand. You say you wanted me to hurt your husband?'

'No, of course I didn't. I thought . . . well, that you and I . . . ' She gave up, embarrassed.

Once again, she saw the dawning comprehension on his face. 'You think . . . I was . . . I did . . . But I have girlfriend. In Portugal. We get married next year. I couldn't — '

'Oh, no, Antonio. Of course I didn't

think that. Why, I'm almost old enough to be your mother.' It didn't do much for her embarrassment, and certainly not for her ego, when he nodded in agreement.

'But I never make you to think — ' His struggles with both the language and the sentiment were excruciating.

'I know you didn't. It was all my fault,' she said quickly. 'I was reading something into a situation when all you were doing was being kind. But tell me, what did you mean when you asked me to meet you in the park the other day? What was all that about?'

'I was going to show you some self-defence moves,' he said. 'So that man would not hurt you again. That was why I wanted to see him, so I could see how big he was. How best to tell you. That was all.'

But beneath all her embarrassment was a deep, deep relief. 'That was very kind of you,' she said. 'And I can only say how very sorry I am for being so — so foolish.'

'No, not foolish, Is-so-bella. You are very kind lady. Very sad too. You helped me so much. I am grateful. And you know, you should not stay with a man who does bad things to you. You are lovely lady. Deserve better.'

'Thank you, Antonio.' She stood up. 'I wish you and your fiancée all the very best. And I don't think I'll be seeing you again. But good luck. And — and thank you again.'

She walked out of the coffee shop with her head held high. In her mind she could hear Bradley's scathing voice, taunting her. But this time, the difference was she didn't listen.

* * *

'What's he up to, Conor?' Elsie asked, her bright blue eyes sharp and intelligent. She looked much better, and when he got to the ward had been awake and only too eager to talk.

'I'm almost there,' he said. 'I'm pretty sure I know the scam Bradley was up to his neck in. The problem is, do I go to the police now, or wait for the last few pieces to fall in to place?'

'It's something to do with Jubilee Terrace, isn't it?' she asked shrewdly. 'I must say, he was in one hell of a hurry to present me with that notice to quit, which my son says is not legally enforceable.'

Conor nodded. 'I took a call this morning from a man I believe to be Martin Sheringham. Does the name mean anything to you?'

Elsie shook her head. 'Can't say it does. Who is he?'

'He's a property developer, among other things. I've done some research on him and found that he's amassed a small fortune, but also a reputation for being a man who sailed a bit close to the wind over the years. His acquisition of Stoneford Manor being a case in point.'

'Stoneford Manor? That lovely old place that's now a posh sports centre?'

'That's the one. He got the property

at a ridiculously low price when the family, struggling to pay off crippling death duties and in a not very good place emotionally, had virtually given the place away.'

'I remember when the sale went through. It was very sad to see a house that had been in the family for generations being sold off. But better than being turned into a housing estate, I suppose. What's that got to do with Jubilee Terrace, though?'

'I'm pretty sure the same man is behind the attempt to buy the properties in Jubilee Terrace. Including Granny Maguire's house.'

Elsie scowled. 'It was wicked, what happened to poor Dora. She was a lovely lady even though I didn't know her very well. Kept herself very much to herself.'

'More the pity. Maybe if she'd had someone to confide in, she'd have dealt with it better instead of worrying herself to death over it,' Conor said and he told Elsie how Den Uppington had tricked her into signing what she thought was an agreement to buy when it fact it was a rental agreement.

'And I'm thinking now it's linked to the Old Founders School. I've been told there was once an attempt by a supermarket chain to buy the property but that they never succeeded because local people got together to buy the building and save it from demolition.'

'Yes, I remember. Lauren's mother was very involved in that. And you think Bradley Northcott had been buying up the shares of those original owners?'

'I'm pretty sure of it.'

'But Lou would never have sold her share, not in a million years,' Elsie said. 'She was a very principled woman. If she believed in something, she believed wholeheartedly.'

'As soon as I get that last piece of the jigsaw, I'll be off to the police with it. You see, I don't think there was ever a deed of transfer when Lauren's mother died. And I think Bradley was trying to trick Lauren into signing it, not

302

realising what she was signing away. After all, they were both L. E. Chapman, weren't they?'

'Yes. It caused no end of confusion, I can tell you. But Lauren would never sign that.'

'Not knowingly, of course. But Bradley was being very clever. I found a stack of papers on his desk the morning after the attack. He'd already asked Lauren to come in early and sign some papers as company secretary. The ones on his desk were just straightforward statutory stuff. But I think he intended to slip the share transfer in among those papers and could be pretty sure she wouldn't read each and every one of them. Particularly if he was standing over her, hassling her.'

'So where's the share transfer now?' Elsie asked.

'I have no idea. It certainly wasn't on the desk or the Stag Holdings file that Bradley's wife gave to me this morning.'

'You don't think . . . ' Elsie's eyes widened.

'I certainly do. I think Bradley's attacker took the paper. As to why, who knows?'

Elsie leaned back against the pillows, deep in thought. Conor glanced at his watch. 'I'll go to the police tomorrow morning. I've said I'd meet Lauren in the Nag's Head at 5 o'clock.'

'You'd better go, then. The traffic on the bypass can be murder this time of night. Good luck, and tell Lauren I'm fine and that I'll take Dooley off her hands tomorrow.'

Elsie's prediction was right. The traffic was indeed building up on the bypass and he sat in the car, frowning, cursing a set of traffic lights that seemed to have been created with the express purpose of bringing the traffic in the town grinding to a halt as quickly as possible. He drummed his fingers on the steering wheel and checked his watch for the fifth time in as many minutes. If he didn't get to the Nag's Head by 5 o'clock, he had no doubt at all that she'd go ahead without him.

Thank goodness he'd made her promise not to, he thought grimly as he hurried across the hospital car park. She was going to be as surprised as he was when she learned the truth.

It was, in fact, almost quarter past five when he finally reached the Nag's Head. The main bar was a bit busier than it had been earlier, with early-evening drinkers calling in for a quick one on their way home from work. But there was no sign of Lauren. Or Dooley.

Keri was behind the bar. She was chatting in her easy flirtatious way with the man Conor recognised as having been with Lauren. Scott Wilde.

Keri looked up as he approached and gave him a big beaming smile. Scott gave him a deep scowl.

'Have you seen Lauren this evening?' he asked. 'I'm supposed to be meeting her here at 5 o'clock, only I got held up in traffic.'

'Not the most patient of people, is your Lauren? Is she, Scott?' Keri asked, and Scott shook his head.

'She'll be long gone,' he said. 'You've been stood up, mate.'

'No, it wasn't like that,' Conor said quickly, only too aware that Scott was a good six inches taller and two stone of solid muscle heavier than him. 'We were meeting up to go and — and see someone. To do with work. She promised to wait for me.'

Scott sniggered. 'She promised, did she? Where were her hands when she made this promise?'

'What?' Conor shrugged. 'I don't know. Oh wait, yes I do. She was fiddling with the dog's lead.'

Scott and Keri exchanged grins. 'It's an old trick of hers,' Scott said. 'She reckons if you cross your fingers behind your back when you make a promise, then it doesn't count.'

'She was always pulling that stunt at school,' Keri said. 'Used to drive us mad.'

Conor's blood froze in his veins. Then he began to run towards the door. He really, really hoped he was wrong, and he didn't give a toss if he was just about to make the biggest eejit of himself.

But he had the feeling Lauren was about to do something that could well put her in grave danger.

22

'Good afternoon, Mrs Northcott,' the nurse at the desk said as Isobel walked into the ward. 'I tried to call you, but you must have already been on your way here.'

'Is it bad news?' Isobel asked anxiously.

'Oh no, quite the contrary. It was to say that your husband has regained consciousness and, considering the nature of his injury, looks to be in great shape with no ill effects whatsoever. Apart from a very sore head, of course. It's quite remarkable. He's one very lucky man. If Mr Murchison hadn't been around when he was brought in, it could have been a very different story. As it is, with luck, he'll soon be back to his old self again.'

'That's great news,' Isobel said. 'Can I go and see him?'

'He's got someone with him at the moment. But as soon as he goes, yes, of course you can.'

Isobel sat on one of the plastic chairs underneath posters inviting you to give blood and not to forget your flu jab, and waited. So Bradley had come round, had he? With no ill effects, by the sound of it. And he'd be back to his old self again, would he? She grimaced at the thought. But it was good news though. The very best.

The door to the side room opened, and a middle-aged man with close grey cropped hair and steely eyes came out. He walked past her without recognising her. But she recognised him. It was the policeman who'd come to see her the day of Bradley's accident.

She took a deep breath and went in to Bradley's room. He was sitting back against the pillows, his face as grey as the washed-out bedcover. 'How are you feeling?' she asked.

'How do you think I'm feeling?' he snarled.

Oh yes, Isobel thought. The nurse was quite right. He was indeed back to his old self. Which just made her next step even easier. 'Was that the police I saw leaving?' she asked. 'Have they found out who attacked you yet? Or have you remembered?'

'They couldn't find the skin off a rice pudding,' he said. His voice seemed to have set in permanent snarl mode. 'Not that it matters. Because I know who it was.'

'You do? Well, who was it? I assume they're on their way to arrest him?'

'No, because I didn't tell them. I just said I couldn't remember anything.'

She looked at him, eyes wide with astonishment. Maybe he had suffered some brain damage after all. 'But why on earth would you do that? You can't let him get away with that. He could have killed you.'

'Let's just say I prefer to keep my powder dry on that one.' He gave her a sly look that she knew well. It meant he was up to something.

'But surely — '

'Just shut up and listen,' he snapped. 'This is important. There's something I need you to do for me. Urgently. There's a file in my bedside drawer. It's just some boring legal stuff. But I want you to get it out of the house.'

'And put it where? In the office safe? You'll have to give me the combination to do that.'

'No, that won't do.' His eyes were darting about, like he was thinking frantically. 'Just — oh, I don't know. My head still feels like it's full of cotton wool. Just use your initiative. I know. Your locker at the country club. Yes, that's the place. Put it in there.'

'But why? I don't understand — '

'You don't need to understand,' he growled. 'But if you must know, the police have got some daft idea in their heads, probably put there by that idiot Conor, that I'm mixed up in some — let's say some financial irregularities. They're talking about getting a search warrant. A fine way to treat someone who's in hospital. But these things take time. So if you could go on home now, you'll be there and gone long before they arrive.'

'Financial irregularity?' She put on an innocent face. 'But surely, Bradley, you haven't done anything . . . irregular, have you?'

'Of course not,' he snapped. 'And Isobel, if you're thinking of doing anything silly, let me remind you that this is your financial future that could be in jeopardy, as much as mine. Do you understand?'

'Yes, of course I do,' she murmured. 'I understand only too well. So is there anything else you'd like me to put in my locker while I'm at it?'

'Well, there are a few items in my study that I'd prefer they didn't get their grubby little mitts on. There are a couple of black leather-covered notebooks in the top right-hand drawer of the desk in my study. It's just a few personal items that I've noted down over the years. You know how I like to keep account of everything.'

'I do indeed,' she murmured, remembering the monthly quiz over the credit card statement.

'Yes, well, you know what the police are like. Any excuse to frame a decent law-abiding citizen and they'll do it just to bump up their crime figures. You wait till I'm back on my feet again. I happen to know some very influential senior police in the Freemasons. That sergeant can kiss goodbye to his pension, and that's a promise.'

'You're looking a bit agitated, Bradley. I don't think that's very good for you in your present condition.'

'Then don't sit there like an idiot gawping at me, woman. Go on home and do what I ask.'

She stood up to go. 'Of course I will,' she said quietly. 'Don't worry about that. I'll see to it that your file and notebooks end up in the right place. You have my word on it.'

Something about the tone of her voice must have alerted him. 'Isobel?'

he said urgently. 'You're not going to do anything stupid, are you? Because if you do — '

'Stupid? Oh no, Bradley. I'm not going to do anything stupid.' Then she turned and walked away.

The nurse looked up as she went past and smiled. 'He's looking remarkably well, isn't he?' she said.

Isobel thought that maybe he hadn't looked quite as remarkably well when she left him as he had when she'd arrived. But she kept the thought to herself.

The house felt cold and empty as she let herself in for the last time. She went up to her room, took down a suitcase and began packing. She packed some of her clothes, but none of the jewellery that Bradley had given her over the years. She was careful to take only things that were one hundred percent hers.

Then she went into his study, opened the top right-hand drawer and took out the notebooks. She had no idea what they were about, and when she looked through them they were just pages and pages of accounts. Nothing that meant anything to her. She left them in a prominent place on the kitchen table where the steely-eyed police sergeant would be sure to find them. Then she took out paper and a pen and wrote the letter she should have written years ago.

'Dear Bradley,' it said. 'Now that I know you're on the mend, I am leaving you. Please address any further communication, including the divorce petition that we agreed upon, to my solicitor.'

She paused and wondered about saying any more, but thought better of it. It was all behind her now. All those years of bullying and put-downs had undermined her confidence, eroding her self-esteem the way the sea erodes a sandbank. But not anymore. That was in the past. Ahead was her new life in Dorset. Where her friend Jo, her husband, and their lovely hotel were waiting. It was all planned. And she wanted nothing from Bradley.

Jo had all sorts of ideas for extending the hotel. And when Isobel suggested a spa and sports hall along the lines of the one at Stoneford Manor, she and Mark had sounded very enthusiastic. After all, Isobel thought, she was getting into this fitness lark now. And she couldn't help thinking of all those lovely young fitness instructors strutting about the place.

She locked up, posted the keys through the letterbox, and drove away for the last time.

23

The Closed sign was on the door of Peas and Cues when Lauren got there, even though the blind was still up and the door unlocked. Dooley's claws clicked on the worn floorboards as he followed Lauren through the shop and along the corridor that led towards the cleaning cupboard that Den called his office.

Den was cowering behind his desk, his face the colour of putty. He looked like a frightened little boy who didn't want to go to school. He hardly registered the fact that Lauren was there, and Dooley's growl only caused him a slight tightening of his lips.

He was, indeed, a pathetic sight. Lauren felt sorry for him until she remembered the way Elsie's hands shook as she'd shown her the notice to quit from the company owned by

Bradley — and Den.

'I know what you did to Elsie,' she yelled, her good intentions to remain calm flying out of the window as she did so. 'How could you?'

He looked like he was doing an impression of a slowly collapsing deckchair. He stared at Lauren like his eyes were going to pop. Then his shoulders sagged and he slumped forward, his comb-over flopping limply across his face like a dead mackerel.

'Den?' She sat down opposite him, scared he was having a heart attack. 'Are you OK? Do you need a doctor?'

He shook his head, his eyes distant and unfocused. 'That Elsie always was a nosy old bat,' he said in a quiet, toneless voice Lauren had never heard him use before. 'So when you told me you'd seen her outside Bradley's office the morning of the attack, I panicked.'

'She had a notice to quit, for heaven's sake. Thanks to you.'

But he gave no indication of having heard her; just went on in that same weird voice. 'After I left you this morning, I saw her in the window with that yappy little dog of hers.'

'Quiet, Dooley,' Lauren said as the yappy little dog chose that particular moment to show Den just how yappy he could be. She wished she had Conor's way with the dog. She was also beginning to wish that she'd waited for Conor after all before racing around here to confront Den, who was obviously having some sort of breakdown and not making any sense.

'Like I said, she was in the window as I went past,' Den was saying. 'So I went in. I only wanted to talk to her. To find out if she'd seen me that morning.'

'You were there when she fell?' Lauren exclaimed. 'But why didn't you get help? She could have died.'

His head shot up. 'You mean she isn't dead?'

'No thanks to you.'

He sat up straighter and pushed his hair back in place. 'I didn't touch her, you know, whatever she might say. You know what these old people are like. They get terribly confused about things. She tripped and banged her head on the post at the bottom of the stairs. I thought she was dead so I legged it. A man in my position can't afford negative publicity, you understand.'

He didn't look like a frightened schoolboy anymore, but more like the bully on the school bus who'd to take the younger kids' lunch money. Lauren stared at him.

'Do you have any idea what becoming mayor means to me?' he hissed. 'To have people treat me with a bit of respect, instead of a figure of fun? I've heard them sniggering behind my back. And you. Don't think I haven't heard you. Because I have.'

Lauren considered telling him that maybe people would start taking him more seriously if he did something about his hair, stopped dressing like Toad of Toad Hall and gave up on the rubbish jokes. But then she figured he probably was not in the mood for lifestyle advice, however well-intentioned.

'As for Bradley,' he went on, 'it was his idea I went on the council. In fact, he fixed it for me via some of his Freemason cronies. Reckoned it would be a good idea to have someone on the inside when it came to planning matters. And once I'd done that and passed on information that with hindsight I realise I shouldn't have, he blackmailed me. Getting me to do all sorts of things, including letting you go and work for him.'

'He did?' Lauren felt a frisson of pride. Was she really that good that Bradley had been forced to resort to blackmail to get her to work for him? 'Surely he could have got someone just as good as me via more conventional recruitment methods?'

'Good?' Spite glittered in his narrowed eyes. 'He didn't want you because you were good, you stupid woman, but because your signature is damn near identical to your mother's. He saw it on my desk one day. You'd filled in some forms for me and he realised that he could get your mother's original shares in Stag Holdings, the company that was formed to buy the Old Founders School, transferred to us without anyone — least of all you and your dad — being any the wiser. He said he'd spun you some yarn about training you up to be company secretary.'

Lauren swallowed hard. Bradley Northcott had reeled her in like the prize idiot she was.

'He did, didn't he? I can tell by your face,' Den smirked. 'He was going to give you a load of boring official forms to sign and slip the deed of transfer in with them. Said you wouldn't realise what you were signing. And that would have been the end of Jubilee Terrace.'

'So that's what it was all about. Elsie said something about starter homes. Is that the plan?'

'That was the original idea, for sure. Demolish the Old Founders School, using part of Jubilee Terrace as the access road. And there you have it. Affordable housing for local people. A sure certain vote-winner for me with an election coming up next year. But then Bradley got involved with this developer guy who had other plans. To build a supermarket, of all things. Like I'm going to agree to that. But they are, it seems, offering silly money.'

'But what had that to do with my mother? Don't say she was involved in anything iffy. I simply wouldn't believe it.'

Den snorted. 'Of course she wasn't. She was as straight as a die, more the pity. But she was one of the original Stags, the action group formed years ago when a supermarket threatened to move into town, back when she had her craft shop. Worked like a Trojan, in fact, and was thrilled when we saw off the supermarket. Victory for the little people, she said.'

'That sounds like her,' Lauren murmured.

'Over the years,' Den went on, 'we

bought out the other Stags, but your mother refused to sell. Some sentimental twaddle about how she'd always wanted to be a shareholder, even if it was, as she believed, in a defunct company.'

'Which it wasn't?'

Den grinned. 'Anything but. Over the years we'd used Stag Holdings as a cover to buy and sell properties. Made ourselves quite a tidy nest egg. So much so that when I've had my turn as mayor, I shall be shaking the dust of this place off my feet and following the England cricket team around the world, faster than you can say *howzat*.'

'So what happened between you and Bradley?'

'A difference of opinion. Demolishing Jubilee Terrace for low-cost homes for local people would be a smart move, politically speaking. But a supermarket? Political suicide. I told Bradley that I'd had enough and wanted to call it quits. But he said he'd get me kicked off the council if I backed out.' He adopted his best party political voice. 'I couldn't permit that. I did it for the good of the town. And this time, I'm the one holding all the aces, because look what else I got. I scuppered his dirty little game, good and proper.'

He took a sheet of paper out of the desk drawer and pushed it across the desk to her. It said 'Deed on Transfer' on the top, and she could see her mother's name on it. She could also see spatters of dark brown on it and had an instant flashback to the moment she'd walked into Bradley's office and found him slumped across the desk.

She sent a mop and bucket cluttering over and Dooley into an excited frenzy as she pushed her chair back and stood up. She stared in horror at the man she'd always thought of as a harmless idiot. *She* was the idiot for having taken so long to make the connection.

'It was you, wasn't it?' Her voice came out as a croak. 'You whacked Bradley over the head with that doorstop, didn't you?'

'Clean bowled,' he said with a proud smirk. 'He never knew what hit him.'

'B-But why?'

'We'd had this up and downer on the phone first thing. He put the phone down on me, so I went round to see him. He didn't hear me because he was on the phone to his developer mate. Laughing, saying how he'd set me up as the patsy. That's what he called me. The patsy. That's when I knew I had to stop him. But I played fair. I gave him one last chance to back down and stop all this nonsense. Told him I wanted out. But he just laughed in my face and told me to go away. So I pretended to do just that. Only, I didn't.'

Lauren held her breath. 'What did you do?' she whispered.

Once again, that self-satisfied smirk. 'I always said what a good left arm swing bowler I was, didn't I?'

'You did?' Lauren just stared at him. 'But I don't see — '

'You don't, do you?' He chuckled as if he'd just made one of his rubbish jokes. 'Well, I stood in the doorway. He had his back to me and didn't know I was there, and I bowled that doorstop as straight and true as they come. Smack dab into the back of his head. And whack, down he went. Clean bowled. Did you know, by the way, that old accountants never die? They just lose their balance. Get it? Poor old Brad lost his balance all right, and then some.' Then he laughed. Not his usual laugh, but a high-pitched whinny that sent a shiver down Lauren's already shivery back.

'But he's not dead.' She bit back the rising nausea as she spoke.

'As good as.'

'No. Conor went to see his wife yesterday and said the surgeon was cautiously optimistic that he'll make a full recovery. Isn't that good news?'

'Good news?' His eyes were small and frightened again. 'Are you mad? He'll say I did it. Of course it's not good news. Here, what are you doing?'

'Phoning the police, of course.' She

took her phone out, but he reached across the desk and grabbed it before she had chance to pull away, moving with a speed she wouldn't have thought him capable of.

'I can't let you do that,' he said. 'Not after what you know.'

'Then what are you going to do? Kill me?'

Oh, how she wished she hadn't said that, because he just nodded and said 'Of course' in a matter-of-fact way as if they were discussing the price of potatoes. Then he picked up a crowbar he used for opening crates. He tapped it against one hand, like he was about to open the batting for England, and advanced towards her.

24

'But think about it, Den,' she said, her voice soft and coaxing. 'So far, no one's been hurt. Bradley and Elsie are both going to be OK. Chances are, this will all blow over and everything will go back to the way it was.'

To her intense relief, he lowered the crowbar. 'You reckon?' he said.

'Of course,' she lied. 'And next time someone says you're a rubbish bowler, I'll tell them — '

Wrong. Wrong. Wrong. Why did she always say stupid things when she was nervous? Her dad was always telling her it was going to get her in big trouble one of these days.

And the look on Den's face as he and his crowbar stood between her and the door was about as big as it gets.

'Come on, Den.' She tried the coaxing voice again. 'You don't want to hurt me. What have I ever done to you?'

'Apart from laugh at me?' He began tapping the crowbar against his palm again. 'And that thing you used to do with the tomatoes really bugged me.'

Getting sacked for a few soggy tomatoes was one thing. Getting killed for them quite another.

She grabbed the fallen mop and lunged at him, catching him so hard in the stomach it knocked the wind out of him for a moment and the crowbar clattered to the floor. She made a run for the door, but in doing so tripped against Dooley, who, thinking they were going somewhere exciting, was running round in circles, barking his head off.

As Den recovered and made a lunge at her, Dooley launched himself at him. His razor-sharp teeth connected mid-thigh, at the point where Den's tight trousers were at their tightest. There was a ripping sound that was almost drowned out by Den's roar of pain and rage. Next thing, Dooley went flying across the room and crashed against the wall with such force a framed picture of Somerset County Cricket Club 1983 fell on him. But the little dog didn't move.

Lauren forgot about Den and his crowbar. She forgot about the danger she was in. All she could think about was poor little Dooley. She felt, rather than saw, Den standing behind her, looking down at them. Felt, rather than saw, his arm holding the crowbar raised. Felt, rather than saw, his momentary hesitation.

'You've killed him,' Lauren screamed. But she was talking to an empty room. Den had gone.

As she bent over Dooley and tried to think if it was possible to do CPR on a small wiry-haired dog, she heard Den's footsteps crashing along the corridor towards the shop. Then Dooley's little chest heaved and he jumped to his feet, his eyes shining as if eager to go back at Den and have a go at the other trouser leg.

'Oh, Dooley, you little darling.' She hugged him to her, tears of relief streaming down her face. But Dooley didn't do hugs or sentimental outpouring, and all she got in return was a shrill yelp of protest so close to her ear it made her let him go.

She followed Dooley out of the storeroom, intent on catching Den before he could get away — and straight into a pair of arms that grabbed her and held her so close she couldn't move. She pushed against him in panic, trying to free her arms. If Den was going to kill her, she was going to get a few well-aimed punches in first.

'It's all right. It's all right. I've got you. You're safe now.' Conor's soft Irish voice was the sweetest sound she'd ever heard.

She heard a howl of anguish as Scott rugby-tackled Den to the floor, sending crates of apples and cabbages off in all directions. Maybe, on reflection, Den's groans, muffled by the weight of Scott's not inconsiderable frame pinning him to the floor, sounded just that little bit sweeter.

'Oh Conor,' she said as the relief kicked in, her knees turned to water and she sagged against him.

'Are you OK?' he asked. 'Did that — that monster hurt you? Because if so — '

'No. No. He hurt Dooley though, but he — '

She got no further as she remembered the moment when, just for a second, she had braced herself for that crowbar to come crashing down on her head.

'I was so scared,' she admitted, as she buried her face in his chest, so close she could feel the thudding of his heart. 'I — I thought — '

She shrugged. For once in her life, Lauren was clean out of words.

Conor stared at her, his eyes intent. Then he gave a small groan, like a man who could not help himself. He bent his head towards her and kissed her very lightly on the lips.

She forgot about Den. She forgot about Dooley. She even forgot to breathe as her whole being focused on this one precious moment. It felt to Lauren that she'd just come home without even realising she'd gone away. She was where she needed to be. In Conor's arms.

She reached up and put one hand on the back of his head where her fingers touched the thick dark hair at the back of his neck. She heard his soft intake of breath as she drew him towards her and kissed him back. But this was no gentle 'are you OK' kind of kiss. This was a 'glad to be alive, isn't life wonderful' kiss. The sort of kiss she'd been waiting all her life for. As if —

'Can someone come and sort this damn dog out?' Scott's angry voice roared, and Lauren and Conor sprung apart like a pair of kids caught with their hands in the biscuit jar. They hurried into the shop, where Scott had Den pinned to the ground among scattered heaps of potatoes and cabbages. Dooley danced around the pair of them like a hyped-up boxer waiting to land the killer punch.

'For goodness sake,' Den bleated, 'that mad dog is going to kill me. Get him away. And let me get up.'

Lauren grabbed Dooley and clipped on his lead. Den struggled to his feet. 'Look, this has all been a terrible misunderstanding, guys,' he said. 'I don't know what she's been telling you, but she's quite mad. I only employed her out of pity.'

'Shut up,' Scott growled. 'Otherwise I'll sit on you again.'

'You could have killed Dooley,' Lauren said. 'I've a good mind to let him go at you again.'

'I wish I had now,' he growled. 'Wish, too, I'd finished you off while I had the chance.'

Lauren's stomach heaved as the memory of that heart-stopping moment when she fully expected to feel the full weight of that crowbar come crashing down on her head rushed back.

'She never shuts up, you know,' Den went on, looking at Scott. 'I tell you now, you won't put up with it like I did. Marry her if you insist, but don't say I didn't warn you. Nag, nag, nag.'

'I'm not staying here to listen to this rubbish,' Lauren said. 'I'll wait for the police outside. Come on, Dooley.'

The truth was, she was feeling quite queasy and needed the fresh air. She leaned against the wall of the shop and took several deep breaths.

'Are you sure you're OK?' It was Conor who'd followed her out. Only he wasn't looking at her in quite the way he had been a few minutes ago, back in the corridor. His eyes, which had been soft, were now hard and narrowed; his mouth no longer softened by a gentle smile but set in a firm, angry line.

'Just needed some fresh air,' she said. 'Shouldn't you be in there, riding shotgun with Scott?'

'Oh, I think your boyfriend's got him well and truly covered,' he said.

'So how come you're both here?'

'Scott was in the Nag's Head, where you'd promised to wait for me.' Conor's voice was as cold as his eyes. 'And explained to me this old, and I have to say extremely childish, trick you have of crossing your fingers when you make a promise so that it doesn't count. A piece of stupidity that could have cost you your life.'

She shuddered. 'Den was Bradley's attacker. I should have twigged. The morning of the attack, when I went in to the office early, I noticed he hadn't opened up, which is unusual. And as for poor Elsie, that was down to him as well.'

'I know all that,' Conor said. 'The police have a warrant to search Bradley's house which I've no doubt they're doing right now. And the file Isobel gave me is going to send both him and Bradley down for a very long time. I've also been in touch with the Institute and they'll be setting up their own investigation into Bradley's wrong-doings. I've said I'll stay until it's all sorted.'

'And then — ?' she asked, hardly

daring to breathe. 'Will you be going back to London?'

He nodded. 'Probably. I hope things work out for you and Scott. He's a good guy.'

'Yes, but we're not — '

But her words were drowned out by the blessed sound of the police sirens. And of course Dooley, who'd found something new to bark at.

By the time she'd given her statement, Conor had gone.

25

'So, Lauren, you're finally off,' Elsie said. 'Dooley and I will miss you.'

'And I'll miss you both. But I'm only going to Bristol. It's not like I'm going to the other end of the country.'

'Or to Ireland,' Elsie added.

'Or to Ireland,' she said with a sigh. 'But I'm glad it's all turned out all right. The new and legal owners of Stag Holdings have given you a life interest in your house, which means you can never be threatened with eviction ever again.'

'And Jubilee Terrace will not be demolished and turned into starting homes.'

'No starting homes,' Lauren said with a smile as she thought how much she was going to miss Elsie. 'And isn't that the best news about the Old Founders School? Not being demolished either, but restored and turned into a boutique hotel.'

Elsie sniffed. 'Whatever that might be. Not sure what your mother would have made of that.'

'She'd have been delighted the place has been saved from demolition. And even more delighted that a smart, trendy new hotel could well be just what Stoneford needs. Thanks to Isobel Northcott.'

Elsie sniffed. 'I'm still not sure that's right. She should be standing in the dock alongside that crook of a husband of hers.'

'But Conor said it was her intervention that had set the police on to the true scale of Bradley Northcott's wickedness. That and the fact that Bradley had got himself involved with this tough businessman who, when he found out what Bradley was up to, threw him to the wolves and made sure the police knew every last detail of his wheeling and dealing.'

'Nothing more than he deserves.'

'Exactly. But the thing that will really upset him is that, in fact, his wife actually comes out of all this quite well. Although she didn't realise it, as he deliberately kept it from her, she was one of the original shareholders in Stag Holdings and, as the share was acquired perfectly legally, still is. And it's her friends, who own a small chain of boutique hotels in Dorset, who've bought the Old Founders School. It was apparently Isobel's idea.'

Elsie sighed. 'And talking of happy endings,' she said, 'how's Scott?'

'As happy as a pig in primroses, up to his neck in wedding plans. And his dad's already getting excited at the prospect of another addition to the Wilde bunch.'

Elsie looked at her closely, her sharp blue eyes missing nothing. 'And you? How do you feel about that?'

'I couldn't be happier. I've always thought Scott and Keri would make a great couple. Goodness knows he spends enough time in her Dad's pub.

I'm delighted for them.'

'How's your dad doing now? The old gossip Bessie Thompson was only saying the other day that he and that Mavis from the supermarket are getting on quite well these days?'

'I think Mavis realises that the way to my Dad's heart lies in an extra large slice of ham and egg pie, you know.' Lauren laughed.

'So when do you start this fancy new job of yours? A bit of a step up from selling Den's soggy tomatoes, I daresay.'

'I know. Trainee accountant. Who'd have thought it?' Lauren's heart skipped a beat. 'I start on Monday and am more than a little nervous, to be honest.'

'But it's not like you don't have someone there to hold your hand,' Elsie said with a smile.

There was a rap on the door, which set Dooley off until he heard the command. 'Dooley. Sit.'

So he did. At least until Lauren had opened the door to let Conor in.

Lauren would always be grateful to

Dooley for running after Conor that night of Den's arrest. Of giving her chance to force Conor to sit and listen while she spelled out, in words of one syllable, that she and Scott were not, nor ever had been, an item.

Eventually he believed her. And now, as soon as she'd said her goodbyes to Elsie, he was driving her to Bristol to begin her new life, working for the same firm of accountants as he now did. She knew she was going to love it. There were a lot of misconceptions about accountants. How they were all boring and wore pinstripes.

Well, she had first-hand knowledge of that. In or out of his pinstripes, Conor Maguire was anything but boring.

We do hope that you have enjoyed reading this large print book.

Did you know that all of our titles are available for purchase?

We publish a wide range of high quality large print books including:
**Romances, Mysteries, Classics
General Fiction
Non Fiction and Westerns**

Special interest titles available in large print are:
**The Little Oxford Dictionary
Music Book, Song Book
Hymn Book, Service Book**

Also available from us courtesy of Oxford University Press:
**Young Readers' Dictionary
(large print edition)
Young Readers' Thesaurus
(large print edition)**

For further information or a free brochure, please contact us at:
**Ulverscroft Large Print Books Ltd.,
The Green, Bradgate Road, Anstey,
Leicester, LE7 7FU, England.
Tel:** (00 44) 0116 236 4325
Fax: (00 44) 0116 234 0205

LOVE WILL FIND A WAY

Miranda Barnes

Convalescing after a car accident, Gwen Yorke leases a remote cottage on the beautiful Isle of Skye. She hopes to find inspiration there for her career as a rug designer, and wants to decide if she and her boyfriend have a future together. In Glenbrittle, she finds herself drawn to the enigmatic, moody Andrew McIver, and his young daughter Fiona. To Gwen's delight, she and Fiona become close, frequently sketching together. But why is Andrew so unhappy about their friendship?

THE PRINCE'S BRIDE

Sophie Weston

One of three royal brothers in the Adriatic principality of San Michele, Prince Jonas works hard. But after a protocol-ridden evening, he's due some downtime in his beloved forest. Hope Kennard was the daughter of the manor back in England. But she has guarded her heart since her childhood ended in financial scandal. She's just passing through San Michele, before moving on to another country, another job. But then a charming forest ranger appears. And this time, her instincts don't help . . .